GRAVE MISSTEPS

A MADDIE GRAVES MYSTERY BOOK 13

LILY HARPER HART

HARPERHART PUBLICATIONS

Copyright © 2018 by Lily Harper Hart

All rights reserved.

No part of this book may be reproduced in any form or by any electronic or mechanical means, including information storage and retrieval systems, without written permission from the author, except for the use of brief quotations in a book review.

❈ Created with Vellum

1. ONE

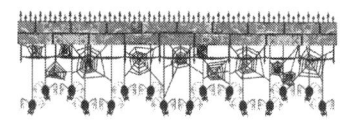

"I've decided I'm twitterpated."

Maddie Graves, her blond hair flying, did a perfect cartwheel. She landed on her feet with a loud thud, raised her hands in the air and did a little bow for her fiancé Nick Winters' benefit. She wore simple cargo pants and a T-shirt – Converse shoes that probably dated back to when they were teenagers – and a broad smile that made Nick's heart completely melt.

"Twitterpated, huh?" Nick had already spread out a blanket and placed their picnic basket at the center of it. He was eager to play as much as Maddie, but he was also lazier in the grand scheme of things and didn't mind relaxing a bit first. "That's what they are in *Bambi*, right?"

Maddie nodded without hesitation. "It's what happens when spring hits and hormones get out of whack."

She was so serious Nick could do nothing but smile. "Well, then I guess I'm twitterpated, too. My hormones are seriously out of whack. Why don't you get over here and fix that?"

Instead of acquiescing, Maddie rolled her eyes. "I think I'm busy doing other things." She performed another perfect cartwheel. "I haven't tried doing one of these since we were teenagers."

"I remember." Nick reached into the picnic basket and pulled out a small stack of wrapped sandwiches. "You fancied yourself an Olympic gymnast at the time, if I recall correctly."

Maddie's smile turned rueful. "Yeah. Even though I'm like eight inches taller than most gymnasts I thought it was a possibility."

"I happen to like how tall you are." Nick was serious. "It makes it easier to hug you without wrenching my back."

"Ha, ha." Maddie wrinkled her nose. "In truth, I was practicing because I thought I might try out for the cheerleading squad." Maddie was embarrassed by the admission. "I didn't tell you because I thought you would laugh at me."

Nick stared at her for a long beat. She was the prettiest woman he'd ever seen in real life – and that wasn't simply because they were getting married in a few months, he really meant it – but she often suffered from poor self-esteem. She was getting better. In fact, over the last year she'd grown in leaps and bounds. He liked to think he had something to do with that but tooting his own horn at Maddie's expense when she was the one who put in all the work seemed like the wrong way to go.

"I knew you were considering trying out for the cheerleading team," Nick said finally, opting for honesty. "I prayed every night before bed that you wouldn't go through with it."

Maddie stilled. "Because you knew I wouldn't make it."

"Because you were just as good as most of the girls – except Phyllis Zimmer who went on to be a cheerleader at Michigan State University, she was at her own level – but you were too shy," Nick explained. "You would've fallen apart at the tryouts. In fact, I remember talking to your mother about it and begging her to forbid you to try out."

Maddie was stunned. "Excuse me?"

"Oh, don't give me that look." Nick made a face. "I was trying to protect you. Your mother understood that. She wouldn't step in, though. She said she thought it was a good idea because you needed to fail ... and in public ... because it would be good for you to face your biggest fear. I remember being really mad at her that day."

Maddie often felt she was mad at Olivia Graves these days. The woman might have birthed and raised her, taken care of her, but she also did a few things Maddie wasn't thrilled with. One of those things was dying, although Maddie couldn't fault her mother for that. It was Olivia dying that brought Maddie back to Blackstone Bay almost a year before. That was also the reason she and Nick reunited and were looking forward to a bright future.

So, while Maddie wasn't happy that her mother died young, she also acknowledged she didn't have a lot to complain about because she had everything she ever wanted ... including her mother. Yes, Olivia Graves might have been dead, but she was still hanging around as a ghost. Maddie's "peculiarity" allowed her to see and talk to ghosts – as well as experience a psychic flash or two when times were tense – and she spent her younger years hiding her secret from everyone (including Nick) to the detriment of her own emotional growth. As soon as she returned to Blackstone Bay and constantly kept running into Nick, she found she could no longer hide the truth and he accepted it with more grace than she would've thought possible.

Oh, Nick was angry, too. His fury stemmed from his best friend abandoning him after high school, though, and not the fact that Maddie was different. He convinced himself that he hated Maddie ... even though, in reality, his heart ached for her. Their reunion was tense and full of strife. Then it turned glorious because they no longer had obstacles in their way. In short order, they declared their love and moved in together. Nick proposed over Christmas and they were currently planning for a summer wedding.

Everything was perfect, including the return of Maddie's father George. He hadn't been around during her younger years – due to a multitude of reasons – but he was trying to make it up to Maddie now. He still traveled for work, but he was making Blackstone Bay his home base so they could spend time together. After initially being leery, Nick was onboard with the situation because he trusted George wanted to do the right thing. So far, things were working out well. That didn't mean Maddie wasn't occasionally snippy with Olivia's ghost for purposely cutting off contact with George. That was the one relationship that still needed smoothing over.

"My mother never said anything to me about trying out for cheerleading," Maddie admitted, chewing on her bottom lip. "I wonder why."

"Probably because she wanted you to make your own decisions."

"Or because she knew I would make a fool of myself and she thought it might be funny." Maddie's expression turned dark. "That's probably it."

Nick didn't bother to hide his eye roll. "I doubt very much that's it. In fact, I think it's a little mean to cast aspersions on your mother that way. I know you're still angry about the George situation, but Olivia was a good mother to you."

"Except for the fact that my father kept showing up wanting to see me and she wouldn't allow it because she was bitter and selfish."

Nick bit back a sigh. Maddie kept waffling back and forth on this topic, her emotions careening from one end of the stratosphere to the other. One second, she forgave her mother for everything and wanted them all to be one big happy family. In the next second she was furious with Olivia and didn't want to talk to her. Nick found the whole thing aggravating because, in general, Maddie's moods were fairly even. He didn't enjoy the constant up and down of late.

"Mad, we've talked about this." Nick kept his tone calm and placating. "Olivia made mistakes and she recognizes that. I thought you were going to try and move past it."

"I am."

"Then go back to being twitterpated," Nick suggested. "I like watching you do cartwheels. It would be more fun if you were in a cheerleading skirt – we'll have to look at buying one of those – but I can learn to compromise."

Maddie made an exaggerated face as Nick fought the urge to kiss her senseless. "That is so not funny."

"I think it was a lot funny."

Maddie did another cartwheel, this one a bit wobblier than the others, and her expression was thoughtful when she returned to her stance. "I never made it to the point where I would get embarrassed by not making the squad. I hid in the girls' locker-room for two hours until the tryouts were over with. I panicked when I was in there because I knew Marla was on the squad and she would never allow me to be picked."

Marla Proctor was Maddie's high school nemesis, although it was all on Marla's part because Maddie did her best not to engage. Nick despised Marla with everything he had and often protected Maddie to the best of his ability, but even he couldn't save her from everything Marla threw at her.

"I remember that day." Nick took on a far-off expression. "I believe I met you outside the school when you finally got the courage to leave and took you for chocolate malts at the Dairy Queen."

Maddie brightened at the memory. "Hey, that's right. You did take me for ice cream that day."

"I believe I also took you for a walk down to the lake," Nick added. "It was still warm because school hadn't even started yet. It was the run-up to football season so it was late August. I caught you a turtle instead of going to practice like I should have."

"You were the star of the team," Maddie pointed out. "You didn't need to practice."

"The coach thought otherwise."

"The coach was an idiot. I ... ." Maddie broke off when she caught a hint of movement in the trees to her left.

Nick immediately sensed the change in her demeanor and swiveled, scowling when he caught sight of a familiar face picking her way through the sparse foliage. Spring was officially upon northern Lower Michigan, but it would be weeks until the weather was predictable. That meant some of the trees were budding but others remained bare. There weren't a lot of places to hide between the house Maddie and Nick shared and the small field they enjoyed picnicking in.

"Maude," Nick intoned, keeping his expression flat. "Is there a reason you're spying on us from the bushes?"

Maude Graves, Maddie's grandmother, made a face as she moved away from the trees. She was dressed in all black – something that bothered Nick profoundly since he was a police officer – and she had a guilty expression on her face. "How did you know I was here?"

"I think Maddie sensed you," Nick replied.

Maddie shook her head. "I heard her. I thought maybe it was a skunk or something at first. You're not very stealthy, Granny."

"And I don't like it when you call me 'granny'. You know I don't like that."

Maddie's full smile was back in place. "Why do you think I do it?"

"Because you've developed a sadistic streak that is completely unbecoming," Maude replied without hesitation. "I blame Nick."

Nick wasn't surprised by the statement. He was genuinely fond of Maude – and vice versa – but she wasn't above throwing him under the bus to get her way. In fact, she was quite comfortable with it. "And why am I to blame?"

"Because I said so."

"Good to know." Nick took a second look at Maude's outfit and shook his head. "You look as if you're dressed for a covert mission. I don't suppose you want to tell me what you have planned, do you?"

Maude adopted an innocent expression that would only work on people who had never met her. "I have no idea what you're talking about."

"That's ninja garb, Granny," Maddie supplied as she joined Nick on the blanket and dug inside the picnic basket for goodies. "You're very clearly going on a ninja mission with your Pink Ladies."

The Pink Ladies were Maude's social group and they were known for causing mischief and mayhem at regular intervals.

"I am not going on a ninja mission," Maude shot back. "In fact, we're having a very nice evening of tea and book conversation."

Nick marveled she managed to get out the statement with a straight face. "Book conversation?"

"Yes. We've started a book club."

"I see. And what did you read this month?"

"*Any Witch Way You Can* by Amanda M. Lee. It's a timeless story of a family caught on the edge of despair. The great-aunt, the most powerful witch in the Midwest, is trying to keep things together, but her goofy nieces and great-nieces keep working against her. She solves a murder in a tracksuit and even has her own pot field. The books are set in this area and they're fan-freaking-tastic. I think I've found my new spirit animal."

Nick couldn't help being impressed. "That was very good. I almost believed you."

"I don't care whether you believe me or not," Maude shot back. "We're reading the entire series of books and using the witches as inspiration in our war against Harriet Proctor."

"Good to know." Nick grabbed a bag of grapes from the picnic basket. "Does that mean you'll be spending the night elsewhere this evening?" He knew better than most that the Pink Ladies enjoyed adding bourbon to their tea and that generally meant they stayed the night at someone's house, only venturing outside if they could do it on foot.

"Probably." Maude bobbed her head. "We're gathering at Rita Barton's house tonight and it's likely to be a long book conversation."

Nick pursed his lips. "Rita Barton, huh? Doesn't she live one block away from Harriet Proctor?"

In addition to being Marla Proctor's grandmother, Harriet Proctor was also Maude's arch nemesis. It seemed lifelong enemies ran in the Graves family.

"Oh, I think you're right." Maude was back to being innocent. "What a funny coincidence."

"Yes, I'm laughing hysterically inside," Nick drawled. "Do me a favor and don't do anything that requires law enforcement to be called to the scene. I have plans for my day and they don't involve bailing you out of trouble."

Maude's expression was so exaggerated Nick had to hold in a smile. "I never get caught. You know that." She flicked her eyes to the picnic basket. "I see you guys are being lame as always."

"Lame?" Maddie was understandably offended. "We're having a picnic."

"And that's lame. You should be out having crazy adventures ... or at least public sex."

Maddie was mortified. "Granny!"

Maude refused to back down. "What? You're young and ridiculously good looking. Both of you. This is the time to have public sex."

"We'll take that into account," Nick said, rubbing his hand over Maddie's back as he tried not to laugh at Maude's gregarious attitude. "As for being lame, we're fine with it. In fact, we're twitterpated."

Maude blinked several times in rapid succession. "Is that some sort of weird sex thing I've never heard about?" she finally asked. "Wait, I know everything about sex. That can't be it."

Maddie was officially at her limit. "It's not that, Granny. It's when it's spring and you're in love. I mean ... basically. That's how we're using it."

Nick cast her a sidelong look. "That's not exactly how you described it to me a few minutes ago. You said it's what happens when hormones get out of control."

"She doesn't need to know that."

Maude snorted. "Well, at least you're having some fun." She offered a half-wave as she turned to go. "I'm only here because I didn't want you guys waiting up for me. I'll be gone all night."

"Thank you for telling us," Nick said. "Don't get arrested."

"Be careful," Maddie called out. "It's still cold at night, so if you decide to vandalize Harriet's house after you get drunk, make sure you wear a hat."

Maude made a clucking sound with her tongue. "Lame, lame, lame."

Maddie waited until she was sure Maude was out of earshot to speak. "We're not lame, are we?"

Nick smirked as he tucked a strand of hair behind her ear. "I don't think so. I don't really care what other people believe, though. I happen to be happy with the way this is all going. If picnics are lame, love, I don't want to be one of the cool kids."

Maddie giggled, genuinely amused. "Me either." She leaned so she could rest her head on his shoulder. "I'm so glad spring is finally here. I love it when we can get outside. I mean, before you know it, summer will be here. We'll be able to head to the lake so you can catch turtles for me and we'll be able to hike in the woods. I can't wait."

Nick pressed a kiss to her forehead. "Me either."

"It's almost been a year."

"What's almost been a year?"

"Since I came back. In a few weeks, it will have been a year. That's like an anniversary of sorts for us, don't you think?"

Nick shrugged. "We didn't exactly fall into each other's arms when you first came back, Mad. I held out a full two weeks before I realized I was hopelessly in love with you. I think we should celebrate our first date as an anniversary."

Maddie screwed up her face in concentration. "I don't think we really had a first date."

"Of course we did."

Maddie shook her head. "No. We decided we loved each other and that was it. We were essentially tied to one another after that."

"But ... ." Nick racked his brain. "Crap. We didn't have a first date."

Amused, Maddie patted his arm. "It's okay. It all worked out in the end."

"No, I want us to have a first date to tell our kids about," Nick groused. "We need to schedule a first date in the next few days or something."

Maddie was understandably confused. "We've been together a long time now. It's too late for a first date."

"It's never too late for a first date." Nick was firm. "In fact, yeah. We're going to go on a first date as soon as I can plan something. It's going to be magical."

His expression was so serious all Maddie could do was acquiesce. "I think it sounds like a fabulous idea."

Nick gave her a soft kiss. "Just wait until I actually pull it off. I ... ." He broke off, his forehead wrinkling as he lifted his nose. "Do you smell that?"

Maddie shook her head. "What?"

"Smoke. It smells like smoke." Nick's first instinct was to look back at the house they shared. It wasn't visible over the trees, but neither was any smoke. When he turned in the opposite direction, though, he was floored. "Look at that."

Maddie followed his gaze, her stomach lurching when she saw the pillars of smoke billowing over the trees. "What do you think that is?"

"I don't know." Nick held out his hand so she could take it. "We're going to find out, though. Come on."

2. TWO

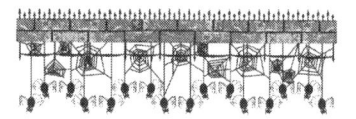

Maddie was in good shape, but Nick's legs were longer and he released her hand once they cleared the trees and could see what was actually happening.

"I have to see if anyone needs help, Mad." His expression was grave. "Call Dale and make sure he gets help out here right away. Tell him to hurry."

Maddie wordlessly nodded as she fumbled in her pocket for her phone. Nick was already running toward the source of the smoke, a large two-story house on the corner of the street. It was rundown, but Maddie knew at least one person lived there, and the occupant was elderly. If she needed help, Nick would provide it ... no matter the danger he found himself in during the process.

Dale Kreskin, Nick's partner on the Blackstone Bay police force, answered on the second ring. "Kreskin," he barked, his tone telling Maddie he wasn't keen about being bothered on a weekend.

"It's Maddie." She was breathless and it took everything she had to concentrate long enough to form words. "The blue house on the end of my street is on fire. Like ... big fire. There's smoke coming through the roof and the building is about halfway engulfed."

Kreskin turned serious. "Where is Nick?"

"Running there now. It's Mildred Wilkins' house. She's ancient ...

although don't tell Granny I said that because I think they're the same age. Nick is going to try and help her."

"Is anyone else there?"

Maddie was frustrated with Kreskin's insistence on asking stupid questions when he should be calling for help. "I have no idea. I can't see. Nick said to send help."

"I've already sent the notice through the system. Fire trucks should be there shortly. I'll be right behind them. I'm just trying to get an idea of what to expect."

Maddie was instantly contrite. "I don't know what to expect." She picked a brisk pace as she walked down the road. She'd lost sight of Nick, but the smoke seemed to be increasing. "If I had to guess, the second floor of the house is on fire. I can't see the main floor or anything else."

"What about the lawn? Do you see anybody on the lawn?"

"No. I don't see Nick either. I think ... I think he went inside."

Kreskin exhaled heavily. "I'm sure he did, too. That is his way, after all. He simply can't stop himself from being a hero."

Tears pricked the back of Maddie's eyes. "I should help him."

"No!" Kreskin's voice was stern. "Nick knows what he's doing. Leave him to do it. You stay outside of that house."

Maddie wasn't keen on being bossed around. "If he needs help, I'm going to help him."

"Of course you are." Kreskin practically growled into the phone. "You be careful, girl. If something happens to you, Nick will never get over it. I just ... be careful. If you were smart, you'd stay outside and let him do the heavy lifting. I'm guessing you're not smart, though."

She knew he didn't mean it as an insult – at least not a really hostile one – but Maddie couldn't stop herself from being annoyed. "I know what I'm doing. You don't have to worry about me."

"I'm on my way," Kreskin barked. "You'd better hope you're safe when I get there."

Maddie disconnected and squared her shoulders as she picked up her pace. She was much more worried about Nick's safety at the present moment than her own. She couldn't shake the feeling that he needed her ... and now.

NICK BANGED ON THE front door, hoping against hope that Mildred would hear the noise and be alerted to the huge problem consuming her house, if she wasn't already. He waited a moment, his ear pressed to the door, and then his instincts took over.

Mildred Wilkins was in her late seventies or early eighties – he couldn't be sure which – and last time he saw her Nick was struck by how much slower she was moving. That was on top of the fact that she needed everything repeated three times to make sure she heard it correctly. That meant he had no idea if Mildred actually heard his banged warning. He also couldn't be sure she was in a position to escape the house.

He tried the door handle, scowling when he realized it was locked. The picture window to the left of the porch was covered by curtains except for a small portion in the center. Nick made his way there, shielded his eyes from the glare of the sun, and peered inside.

Everything was dark, drearily so, but nothing looked out of the ordinary. The house was neat and tidy. It was also empty. There was no sign of Mildred.

Nick took a moment to stare at the road, tilting his head as he waited for the familiar sounds of sirens. If the fire trucks were close, he would wait and allow the trained firefighters to take over the unenviable task of searching for Mildred. He didn't hear anything, though, which made his stomach clench.

The smoke hung over the air like a thick curtain and Nick knew if it was this bad outside it had to even be worse inside. He could see Maddie on the road, the phone pressed to her ear as she hurried in his direction but understood he couldn't afford to wait.

He grabbed the small chair from the front porch and threw it at the window with everything he had, covering his face when the glass shattered. He cast one more look to Maddie – she wasn't looking in his direction – but he could read the worried slope of her shoulders, and then vaulted inside the house.

He couldn't leave Mildred Wilkins to fend for herself. It wasn't in him. He prayed Maddie would recognize the situation was dangerous and opt not to follow him inside. She was often hard to read – and brave to a fault – but she was also smart. She would wait for him where it was safe, perhaps direct the firefighters when they arrived. That would be it.

Even as Nick narrowed his eyes in an effort to see through the gloom, he knew that was wishful thinking. Maddie would follow him because she wouldn't be able to stop herself from doing it. She wouldn't simply be keen to make sure he was okay but Mildred, too. She had a good heart and a courageous soul. He often worried the latter would be the death of him.

"Mrs. Wilkins!" Nick bellowed the name, his eyes watering from the smoke as he looked to the left and the right. He wasn't familiar with the layout of the house but knew it was a colonial, which meant the bedrooms were all on the second floor. Given the sounds coming from above, Nick didn't like that prospect one bit. "Mildred!"

No answer. He couldn't make out anything but splintering wood. If he was going to check the upstairs, he would have to do it now. He was running out of time.

Nick cast one more look over his shoulder before cursing under his breath and heading to the right. He found the stairs right away and tentatively touched the banister. It wasn't hot – which was a good sign – but he worried he would lose his sense of direction once he was completely overtaken by the smoke. Ultimately, that couldn't be helped. He had no choice.

"Mildred!" Nick yelled again as he began ascending the stairs. "Mrs. Wilkins!" All he could do was call her name and hope it wasn't already too late.

"NICKY!"

Maddie found the broken front window almost immediately and

she was beside herself. She covered her mouth but that didn't stop a coughing fit from wracking her body. She'd always been susceptible to smoke. When the other kids experimented with smoking in high school she was the only one who started coughing before inhaling. She'd been embarrassed at the time but was relieved now because she had no doubt she would've turned into a stress smoker if the situation had been different.

As far as Maddie could tell, the house was empty. She was certain Nick went through the window, but she couldn't see him. She was about to climb through the opening and start her own search, but a pair of strong arms grabbed her from behind before she could.

"Don't even think about it, Maddie." Rob Stone, one of Blackstone Bay's longest running volunteer firemen, gave her a hard tug as he pulled her away from the window. "We've got it from here."

Maddie exhaled heavily when she saw the trucks setting up shop on the front lawn, but that didn't stop her anxiety from kicking into overdrive as she struggled to break free of Rob's grip. "Nick is in there."

Rob's eyebrows flew up so far they disappeared under the brim of his hat. "Nick Winters?"

"No, Nick Nolte," Maddie snapped. "He's having another drunken episode."

Rob scorched her with a look. "I'm trying to help."

Maddie realized she was acting out of control and stopped struggling. "I know. I just ... we saw the smoke and Nick told me to call Dale. I did, but he was gone by the time I caught up. This window was broken, which I think means he's inside."

Rob opened his mouth to argue, but he doubted very much that Maddie's assertion was wrong. Instead he changed course. "I'll find him." He was calm as he rested a hand on Maddie's shoulder. "I promise I will."

Maddie balked. "I should help."

"No, you should go over there." Rob pointed her away from the window. "We're here now, Maddie. We have a job to do. You have to let us do it. You'll just get in the way if you poke your head in there."

Maddie wasn't convinced that was true. "He needs me."

"I've known Nick for a long time. In fact, I've known both of you since you were about this high." Rob held a hand to his hip and smiled. "The one thing I can say without reservation is that Nick would want you to stay outside of this house. Your safety is the most important thing to him ... beyond everything else."

She wanted to believe him, but Maddie couldn't stop herself from choking back a sob. "But ... I have to look."

"No, you don't," Nick announced, appearing in the open window. His voice was raspy from the smoke and his face was creased with soot. He was alive, though, and alone. "You stay out there. Rob is right."

Maddie ignored Nick's filthy appearance and bossy words and threw her arms around him. Nick recognized there was no sense admonishing her so he returned the hug even as his body shook with a coughing fit.

"Let's get you out of there." Rob hooked his hand under Nick's arm and helped him through the opening. He remained impassive as Nick sucked in gaping mouthfuls of oxygen, instead waiting until the police officer was in control before asking the obvious question. "Mildred?"

Nick shook his head. "I can't find her. I went upstairs, but it's engulfed. I tried calling for her, although I had no idea what I would've done if she answered. You can't get through to the second floor. Once you get to the top of the steps you're cut off."

"No, getting up there is probably out of the question. The fire is poking through the ceiling." Rob pointed up as a frigid stream of water hit the top of the house, a steady deluge trickling down and hitting Maddie full in the face. She shivered but remained tucked in close at Nick's side. "We should be able to put it out, but if she's not on the first floor then that means she's probably on the second ... and it's already too late."

Maddie's heart skipped a beat. "But ... will you look?"

Rob nodded. "We'll look. I can't guarantee we can get up there either, though."

"We'll get out of your way." Nick hooked an arm around Maddie's shoulders. "We'll be close, though. If you have any updates ... good or bad ... we want to know."

Rob nodded. "Let us do our job. You should probably wear an oxygen mask for a bit, just to be on the safe side." He winked, although the gesture wasn't entirely playful. "Maddie, I'm putting you in charge of that."

Maddie nodded without hesitation. "I've got it. I'll make him do it whether he wants to or not."

"I believe you will."

TWENTY MINUTES LATER, Nick was still getting oxygen and Maddie was busy splitting her time between doting on him and pacing the area in front of the ambulance parked near the end of the long driveway.

That's where Kreskin found them, and he didn't look happy when he caught sight of Nick's filthy features. "You just had to go inside, didn't you?"

Nick shrugged as he attempted to remove the mask, but Maddie slapped his hand away.

"You have ten minutes left under that mask," Maddie ordered. "I plan to make sure you stay here for the duration."

Nick eyed her for a long beat but ultimately nodded. He saw no reason to pick a fight with her when it wasn't necessary. He knew her bossiness stemmed from concern and love so he decided to let it go.

"He has to rest," Maddie explained to Kreskin. "He inhaled a lot of smoke so he has to stay right here and keep that mask where it is." She didn't overtly say that she thought Kreskin might draw Nick to the dark side, but the accusation was splashed clearly across her face.

"I can see you've got your Florence Nightingale impression down pat," Kreskin drawled. "I think Nick is in for a fine time this evening since you've decided to play nurse."

Maddie refused to rise to the bait. "I'm not having this conversation."

Nick put his hand on Maddie's shoulder and gave it a firm squeeze, all the while shooting his partner a warning look. "Leave her alone. She's a little worked up." His voice sounded thick through the mask. "I looked for Mildred inside. I couldn't find her. Rob has men on the lookout, too, but so far they've come up empty."

"Maybe we'll get lucky." Kreskin turned philosophical. "Maybe she's not even here."

Maddie brightened at the prospect. "Do you think that's possible?"

Kreskin shrugged. "I don't know. It would be nice, though. The alternative is a little hard to stomach."

"Yeah." Maddie returned to her pacing, allowing Nick and Kreskin a chance to talk about serious matters as she ran a myriad of possibilities through her head. Most of them were dark, variations on what might've happened if Nick didn't appear in the window when he did, but a few were brighter and she opted to focus on those.

Maddie followed the line of the driveway as she paced, making sure to give the fire trucks a wide berth. She wasn't keen on talking to anyone and was happy to leave Kreskin in charge of Nick's recovery – at least for a few minutes – as she got a better look at the house. In fact, Maddie was so intent on the basement windows, which looked completely normal, that she didn't notice the forlorn-looking ghost staring at her until she was almost on top of her.

"What the ...?" Maddie gasped, dumbfounded. She'd never seen a ghost turn up quite so quickly, although this wasn't a face she recognized. This woman was far too young to be Mildred and not someone Maddie knew from Blackstone Bay. "I ... guess you were in the house, huh?" Maddie felt inexplicably sad. "We tried to get inside but ... I'm so sorry."

The woman waved off the apology and pointed toward the house. She didn't speak. Maddie rationalized that perhaps it was impossible because she was so new ... at least if she died in the fire. She pointed, though, and she was insistent about the direction she wanted Maddie to look.

"What are you trying to show me?" Maddie was confused as she walked a bit, opting to angle closer to the house even though the water cascading down was frigid and likely to cause a chill. "Is there something here?"

She pointed at the basement window.

"Something in the house?" Maddie queried. "I ... oh. Is there a dog in there or something? Is it Mildred?" Maddie dropped to her knees and peered through the window in question, her stomach clenching when a pair of eyes – human eyes – stared back from the other side.

In one brief moment Maddie read everything the trapped individual was feeling, her psychic senses going into overdrive. Fear. Desperation. Hunger. Resignation. Whoever was inside thought he or she was going to die.

In her head, Maddie knew she should call out for help. She didn't, though. She simply reacted. She grabbed a huge rock from the ground, one that was so large it took both hands for Maddie to grip it properly. "Duck your head," Maddie ordered. The window was one of those wavy ones that didn't allow her to get a proper look at the occupant. Ultimately it didn't matter who she was saving, though. It mattered that someone needed help. "Back up just a little and cover your face."

The shape did as instructed and Maddie wasted no time slamming the rock into the glass. It cracked but didn't give so she struck it a second time. The second blow did the trick because the glass cascaded inward and created an opening.

Maddie dropped to her stomach and extended a hand. "Jump up. Grab me. I'll pull you through."

The hand that landed in hers felt small, almost ridiculously so. Maddie tugged with everything she had and pulled the individual through the window. It wasn't until they were both completely clear of the house and rolling closer to the trees to get away from the frigid water that Maddie saw things for what they were.

"Holy smokes! You're a kid."

And at just that moment, the house's roof began to crumble.

3. THREE

Maddie reacted out of instinct and covered the shaking girl with her body, using all her strength to drag the confused young thing away from the house so they wouldn't inadvertently be struck by falling debris when the roof caved in.

"Maddie!" Nick's face was full of terror when he and Kreskin rounded the corner of the house, his eyes going wide when he realized Maddie wasn't alone. "Who is this?"

Maddie shrugged as she straightened, her hand automatically going to the girl's hair to smooth it. Her fingers were immediately caught in huge snarls and now that they were safely away from the house she took a moment to look over the girl's rather rugged appearance. The hair, which Maddie focused on first, was long and brown. It wasn't lustrous like it should be, instead filthy and in desperate need of a trim.

Instead of regular clothing, she wore an ankle-length nightgown that looked to be from decades before. The image on the front of it was faded, but Maddie was almost positive she recognized a *My Little Pony* logo.

The girl's skin was sallow and she refused to make eye contact, her feet bare and toenails overgrown. Out of nowhere, she started shaking to the point where Maddie thought her bones might break from the movements.

"It's okay." Maddie instinctively sat and drew the girl down with her, wrapping her arms around her as she shuddered and made whimpering noises. "You're okay. You're out. You're going to be fine."

Nick moved closer but immediately stepped back when the girl cringed and burrowed closer to Maddie. He recognized the signs of shock right away. There was something more here, too, though. It was something he was loath to put a name to. He exchanged a quick look with Kreskin. "Do you have any idea who she is?"

Kreskin looked as confused as Nick felt. "Not even a little. Where did she come from, Maddie?"

Maddie pointed toward the broken window. "She was in there."

Nick swiveled so he could better see where she pointed. "How did you even see her down there?"

"Oh, well … ." Maddie trailed off and bit her bottom lip. She didn't want to use the G-word around a child in case it sent her over the edge. Kreskin was aware of her ability, but he wasn't a fan of talking about it. Still, she felt she needed to tell the truth. "I thought I saw a friend – which turned out to be true – and she pointed me in the right direction."

"A friend?" Kreskin furrowed his brow and opened his mouth to ask the obvious question.

Nick silenced him with a small shake of his head. "She means a special friend and don't ask about it." He licked his lips and pressed his palm to his forehead. "Did you recognize her?"

"If you're asking if it was Mildred, it wasn't," Maddie replied. "She was … younger. I've never seen her before."

"What did she say?"

"Nothing. She just pointed." Maddie flicked her eyes to the spot where the ghost stood moments before. "She's gone now."

"Okay, well, we'll talk about that later." Nick decided to take charge of the situation. "Sweetheart, can you tell us your name?" He pasted a charming smile on his face as he worked to ingratiate himself.

For her part, the shaking youth didn't as much as glance in Nick's direction. Instead she burrowed closer to Maddie and desperately wrapped her arms around her torso. Maddie soothingly stroked her back, fear momentarily overwhelming her to the point where she realized it was the girl communicating her terror and not something organic from inside of herself.

"It's okay." Maddie kept her voice low. "I ... it's okay. We want to help you. I swear that we don't want to hurt you. We'll make sure no one hurts you." She rocked back and forth, humming lightly as she attempted to ease the girl's discomfort. "We'll take care of you. It's going to be okay."

Instead of relaxing, the girl started a soft keening that threatened to break Maddie's heart.

"Nicky ... ."

"I know, Mad." Nick straightened and motioned for Kreskin to move further back. "I will not be far. You need to stay there, though, and ... well, keep doing what you're doing. We're just going to talk over here."

Maddie didn't like the idea of being cut out of the conversation, but she understood that their options were severely limited. "Okay. I'll stay right here."

Nick met her gaze for a moment, nodded, and then retreated around the corner so he could openly discuss the situation with his partner. "Where the holy heck did she come from?"

"You heard Maddie," Kreskin shot back. "She came from the basement."

"But ... why was she there?"

"I have no idea. She doesn't look healthy, though. In fact, if I had to guess, I would say that she hasn't seen sunshine in months."

"That could technically be true of any Michigan resident over the winter months," Nick pointed out. "The news even did a story about how we didn't see the sun for the entire month of January. I don't know that the kid's lack of a tan can be used as a basis for judgment."

"It's not January. That kid is so pale you can practically see through her. That's on top of being filthy and very clearly mistreated."

Nick balked. "How do you know she was mistreated? I mean ... yeah, she's dirty. I think she looks a little underfed, too. I don't see any bruises on her, though. Of course, we can't get close enough to look."

"We need help with this." Kreskin was firm. "I know you think Maddie is capable of anything, but we need a professional in this particular situation because we are so far out of our depth that I only know one place to start."

Nick eyed him coolly for a long beat. "And where is that?"

"Child Protective Services."

Nick fought to tamp down his distaste. "Do you really want to do that?"

"Do you see where we have any choice?"

Nick leaned so he could look toward the back of the house again, frowning as he watched Maddie rock back and forth. "I guess we don't have a choice. I can tell you right now, Maddie isn't going to like it."

"Yeah, well, I figure that's your problem."

"Thanks so much for that."

"You're welcome."

NICK AND KRESKIN GAVE MADDIE room to engage with the girl, keeping a safe distance away because it became obvious whenever they tried to interact with her that the frightened soul simply was not going to put up with it. She regressed every time she saw them, which made Nick unbelievably antsy as they waited for a social worker to arrive.

In the meantime, he watched the firefighters work. They managed to extinguish the blaze not long after Maddie's discovery, but they were still inside searching for signs of Mildred as they poked and prodded at hot spots that might need further attention.

"Maybe I should tell them to be on the lookout for a younger woman, too," Nick mused after a few moments of silence. "Maddie said the ghost she saw wasn't Mildred. Maybe someone else was living in the house."

"Or maybe Mildred did something to that woman and the kid," Kreskin suggested. "Maybe she set the fire and took off."

Nick cocked an eyebrow. "Do you honestly believe that?"

Kreskin shrugged. "I'm not sure what to believe. I have no idea how that kid ended up in the basement. If you can explain that to me – explain why the kid looks the way she does – I'm more than willing to listen to whatever theory you come up with."

Nick opened his mouth to answer but came up empty. "I don't know. I can't explain any of it."

"Well, neither can I. For now, let's keep the conjecture to ourselves. Here comes Rob. Maybe he'll be able to explain this to us so it makes sense."

Nick was hopeful but doubtful all the same. He lifted his chin as Rob approached. "Anything?"

Rob nodded, his lips curved down. "We found a body."

"What did she look like?"

Instead of immediately answering, Rob furrowed his brow. "What?"

Nick realized his mistake too late to take it back. "I mean ... was it Mildred?"

"Yes. Who else would it be?"

Kreskin heaved out a sigh and grabbed Rob's arm, being careful to keep him from rushing forward as he pulled him to a position where he could clearly see Maddie and the girl. "Maddie found her in the basement."

"What?" All the oxygen whooshed out of Rob's lungs. "But ... how?"

"She saw her through the window," Nick replied hurriedly. "She broke it and pulled her out."

"Why didn't you tell us?" Rob's tone was accusatory. "There could be more kids in there."

"I didn't even think about it," Nick admitted, contrite. "We were too busy dealing with the one kid. She's ... a mess. She hasn't spoken and she keeps crying. She doesn't want men around her either. She only seems to respond to Maddie, and I'm guessing that's because Maddie is the one who pulled her out of the house."

Rob's expression was hard to read, but Nick could imagine the things going through the man's mind. "You think she was abused, don't you?"

"I think she's in pretty rough shape and looks malnourished," Nick clarified. "She didn't have any bruises on her that we could see, although she's pretty well covered. She obviously doesn't want us near her so we've been keeping our distance."

"What are you going to do?" Rob was honestly curious. "You obviously can't let Maddie keep her. It would be hell on your romantic life, for one thing, but I'm also fairly certain it's illegal."

Nick made a face. "I'm not going to let Maddie keep her. Good grief."

"We called Child Protective Services," Kreskin volunteered. "They're on their way. We're out of our depth here. We need help."

"Definitely," Rob agreed, shaking his head as he watched Maddie try to soothe the girl. "As for Mildred, you're going to probably want an autopsy. We found her on the floor. Her body isn't exactly pristine, though. She was identifiable, but you're probably going to want a cause of death."

"That's one of our first orders of business."

SHARON LANSING WAS DRESSED in jeans and a T-shirt, a hoodie wrapped around her diminutive shoulders when she arrived on scene. Nick and Kreskin met her by the road, apologizing for interrupting her weekend before launching into their tale.

"It's okay." She was a brunette, short of stature, but the look she shot Nick was keen with interest. "I wasn't doing anything anyway, just hanging out with some girlfriends." She stressed the word "girl" and offered up a pretty smile.

Kreskin recognized the look on her face and could do nothing but shake his head. "We have a real situation."

"Right. Of course." Sharon shook herself out of her reverie. "And where is the girl you found?"

"Around back," Nick answered.

"She's alone?"

"No, she's with my fiancée."

Kreskin pressed his lips together to keep from belting out a surreal laugh when Sharon's lips curved down. "Maddie is the one who saved her. She's not speaking and she's ... traumatized or something."

"Did you have her checked out by the paramedics?" Sharon was all business now. "That's probably important."

"She doesn't seem to want men around her," Nick replied. "She doesn't like it when Dale and I try to talk to Maddie. I don't think it's going to be easy to separate them." Since he hadn't yet told Maddie what was about to happen, he knew that was doubly true. "I'll go over there now and try to break the news."

Sharon was confused. "To whom?"

"Maddie," Nick replied. "I'll let Dale give you the basics. I'll motion when it's okay to approach."

Sharon didn't look happy with the suggestion but nodded. "Okay. I guess I'll just wait here."

NICK WAS QUIET AND slow as he moved, pasting a wan smile on his face when Maddie lifted her head and met his gaze. She didn't return the smile, instead frowning when she saw the slope of his shoulders.

"You're about to tell me something bad, aren't you?"

Nick stopped when he was still ten feet from the duo, slipping his thumbs into the belt loops of his jeans as he rocked back on his heels. "I'm about to tell you something you're not going to like," he conceded. "We don't have a choice in this, though, so I want you to remain calm for our young friend's benefit."

Maddie rubbed her hand over the girl's back and craned her neck in an attempt to see around the side of the house. She could make out a new figure, one that wasn't very large and who seemed intent on staring in her direction. "Who is that?"

"Sharon Lansing. She's with Child Protective Services."

Maddie immediately balked. "No. What are you thinking?" She managed to keep her voice calm and even, but just barely. "She'll freak out."

Nick's expression was full of sympathy as he stared at the girl. "I know that, but we have no choice. This is above our level of expertise, Mad."

"But ... ."

"No." Nick firmly shook his head. He knew this was going to be a battle but holding his ground was the only option. "Love, you know I would give you anything your heart desires if I could, but I have to follow the rules on this. Mildred was found dead inside. There are some things we have to investigate.

"As for her, well, she needs professional help to deal with whatever happened in that house," he continued. "We're not equipped, Mad. I know you feel attached to her because you found her, but she absolutely has to go with the CPS woman."

Maddie's forehead puckered and, for a brief moment, Nick thought she was going to start crying. He silently hoped against hope that she would pull herself together and stop short and he was relieved when she appeared to do exactly that.

"Fine." Maddie heaved out a sigh and shifted the girl a beat, staring down at the waxen face as the youngster eyed Nick with overt distrust. "Listen, I know you've been through a lot, but if you can speak ... well, now would be the time to do it. We need information from you if you want us to help."

The girl merely growled as she turned her head back into Maddie's chest. The brief look Nick got at her face caused him to wonder as he carefully dropped down to his knees and stared hard at her dirty feet.

"How old do you think she is?" Nick asked finally.

The question caught Maddie off guard. "I don't know. She won't talk. I guess, given her size, I would say twelve or so."

"I think she might be older." Nick desperately wanted to turn the girl's face so he could study her bone structure, but he knew that would be a terrible mistake. "I think she might be fifteen or sixteen."

Maddie stared hard at the girl's thin arms and then shook her head. "She's too small."

"I know, Mad, but I think I'm right." Nick was gentle as he leaned forward. "Honey, we have someone here to help you. You're going to need to come with me, though, because Maddie has to stay here."

He waited to see if the girl would react. When she did, she jerked her eyes away from his face and only clutched Maddie tighter.

"She understood you," Maddie noted. "I think she can talk, but she doesn't want to. At least that's my guess."

"It's mine, too." Nick pressed the tip of his tongue against the back of his teeth. "I'm going to need your help here, Mad. We need to put her in CPS custody and you're going to have to help us do it."

Maddie's heart constricted. "Isn't there another way?"

"No, love. We have to follow the strict letter of the law on this. We don't know who she is or where she belongs. She can't stay here, though."

"But what about taking her … ." Maddie broke off before finishing the sentence. She was going to suggest taking the girl home with them, but she realized right away what a ridiculous idea it truly was.

Nick was happy when he saw the resigned realization slip across her face. "You're going to have to work with me, Maddie. It's going to take both of us."

"What if it traumatizes her, though?"

Nick was afraid it was going to traumatize all of them, but he'd steeled himself for this and refused to back down. "We can only do our very best." He reached out a hand toward the girl. "Honey, I need you to trust me. This really is in your best interests. I promise."

He gathered up his courage and put his hand on her arm. She started screaming immediately, thrashing about so hard she knocked Maddie in the face with her elbow. Nick jumped in to restrain her as Maddie fought back tears, but the girl didn't stop screaming until after she was loaded in the car, a feat that took all of Nick's strength and determination.

Even then, the accusatory glare she lobbed in his direction as Sharon drove away with her in the backseat was something Nick knew he would not soon forget. When Maddie dissolved in tears, he was certain that it would be something she would carry with her for a very long time.

4. FOUR

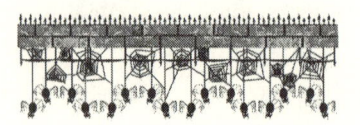

Nick was frustrated by Maddie's reaction to the removal of the girl. She stood a good thirty feet away, her arms folded over her chest, and stared at the house as the firefighters worked inside to make sure the immediate danger was over. She didn't as much as look in Nick's direction.

"Something tells me you're in the doghouse," Kreskin teased, moving to Nick's side and causing him to scowl.

"Something tells me you're right. There was nothing else I could do, though. I mean ...what did she expect?"

"You're preaching to the choir, son." Kreskin was amused despite the serious situation. "I think you did the exact right thing."

Nick dejectedly scuffed the toe of his shoe against the gravel. "Maddie doesn't think that."

"Maddie is still traumatized from that girl being ripped away from her," Kreskin argued. "I think my ears are still ringing from the crying ... and Maddie was louder than the girl in that respect."

"Ugh." Nick rubbed his forehead. "I have to go over there. It's getting dark and her clothes are wet. She can't stay out here."

Kreskin gave Nick a considering look. "You're a brave man. There isn't enough money in the world to make me go over there given the look on her face."

Nick secretly agreed with him. "There's nothing she can do here. I'm sending her home." His shoulders were squared as he approached Maddie, internally cringing when her expression turned darker as he approached. "Love, I think you should head home."

"I don't want to head home." Maddie was firm. "I want to watch what's going on here."

"I know that but ... ."

"I want to see." Maddie's sea-blue eyes flashed with anger. "Are you really going to cut me out of this on top of everything else?"

Nick's temper got the better of him. "I have no intention of cutting you out. As for the girl, you're going to realize I was right about that once you've calmed down. I know you're upset about the screaming ... ."

"And the fingernails cutting into my flesh as you ripped her away from me," Maddie snapped, raising her arm so he could see the discolorations on her skin.

Nick's heart rolled at the sight. "Mad, I'm sorry." He was instantly contrite as he carefully looked over her arm, pressing a kiss to her palm before continuing. "She needs help that we can't give. I'm sorry for how it went down but ... we didn't have a choice."

Maddie's eyes pricked with unshed tears. "I know. I'm sorry. It was just ... hard."

"I know." Nick pulled her in for a hug, smoothing her hair as he rocked back and forth. "We'll check on her as soon as we can. We won't forget about her. I promise you that."

Maddie's sniffle was pitiful. "Okay."

"Okay," Nick agreed, kissing her forehead. "As for the rest, I'm not cutting you out. You're damp, though, from the water they sprayed on the house. I want you to go home and take a hot bath. I'll be there as soon as I can to update you on what we find inside."

Maddie balked. "Why can't I stay with you?"

"You know why." Nick refused to back down. "I have to focus on going through that house and I can't if I'm worried about you. I would really appreciate it if you would go home so I know you're safe. I promise I'll share information as soon as I get it."

Maddie's expression reflected resignation and overt sadness, causing a small tear in Nick's heart.

"Fine." Maddie rubbed the tender spot between her eyebrows. "I'll go home. I'm not going to like it, though."

"Fair enough."

MADDIE FOUND MAUDE and two of her fellow Pink Ladies in the kitchen when she got home. They were brewing tea and cackling like wicked witches looking for a dog and planning for a tornado. Under normal circumstances, Maddie would've found their antics funny. She was far too exhausted to deal with them today, though.

"What are you guys even doing here?"

Maude jolted at the sound of her granddaughter's voice, swiveling quickly and giving Maddie a hard stare. "You look terrible. What happened to you?"

"I thought you said she was out playing with Nick," Rosemary Stevens, one of Maude's oldest friends, said in what she thought was a whisper. "He's the one who probably did that to her hair."

"Ha, ha." Maddie didn't bother hiding her eye roll as she shuffled into the room and grabbed the teapot from the stove. "You didn't put the bourbon right in the water, did you?"

Maude made a face. "Of course not. You can't put the bourbon in first. It will boil away and that's a waste of good bourbon."

"Great." Maddie poured herself a cup of tea and sat at the end of the table, making a face when she realized the third woman in the room – Joni Mason – was licking her spoon and staring at the wall rather than paying attention to the conversation. "What's up with her?"

Maude barely spared Joni a glance. "She's fine. She's contemplating the meaning of life."

Maddie had no idea what to make of the statement. "Is she drunk?"

Maude shrugged. "Who knows what she is. She's just ... Joni."

"Just Joni," Rosemary repeated on a giggle.

"You're all clearly drunk," Maddie groused, shaking her head. "What are you even doing here? I thought you were spending the night someplace else."

"I am, but I needed to pick up toilet paper." Maude was completely guileless. "We don't have enough for our plan. If you're worried about us driving drunk, don't. I'm not drunk. I haven't even had a single drink. That's for after we start enacting our plan."

"Oh, well, as long as you're being safe." Maddie dragged a restless hand through her hair, the events of the afternoon finally catching up with her.

Maude didn't miss her granddaughter's weary expression and she took pause. "What's wrong, Maddie girl? When I left you, I was convinced you and Nick were going to spend the rest of the day saying 'no, you're prettier' over a picnic. What happened?"

"We never even got to the picnic." Maddie jerked her head to the east as something occurred to her. "In fact, we left everything in the clearing. Ugh. It's probably going to attract scavengers."

"So the raccoons will be well fed." Maude was blasé. "It hardly matters. You can go back tomorrow. What happened to interrupt your picnic?"

Maddie told Maude about the fire, leaving nothing out. When she got to the part of the story about rescuing the girl from the basement, all three women were focused and listening.

"It was horrible, Granny." Maddie fought back tears. "She was dirty and she didn't speak. She clung to me as if I were a lifeline. Then the CPS woman showed up and dragged her away. She was screaming ... and clawing ... and I've never felt so helpless in my entire life."

Maude stared hard at Maddie. "Wow. That's quite the story."

"That's all you have to say?" Maddie was incredulous. "I thought you would be as upset as me."

"I don't know what to say." Maude rubbed her forehead. "I just ... that's unbelievable."

"WE FOUND SOMETHING."

Rob met Nick in the living room of Mildred's house and pointed toward a door at the far wall. Nick followed his finger with his gaze and held his hands palms out. "What are you showing me?"

"We found the basement and there's something you should see," Rob replied grimly. "This way."

Nick exchanged a weighted look with Kreskin before following him through the door. The electricity was out so Rob used a flashlight, making sure to carefully illuminate the rickety steps so no one would accidentally take a header down the narrow staircase.

"What is it?" Kreskin asked, eager to break the silence.

"You have to see it to believe it." Rob moved through a dingy room once they hit the bottom floor, stopping in front of another door and lifting his flashlight beam until it landed on a padlock, which happened to be located outside rather than inside. "Do you see this?"

Nick's heart dropped to his stomach. "That girl, whoever she is, was locked down here against her will."

"I would definitely agree with that," Rob said. "She couldn't have gotten out if she wanted to."

Kreskin was horrified. "Mildred did this? But ... why? Why would she possibly want to lock away that girl?"

"I have no idea," Nick replied, giving the lock a tug and frowning when it didn't give. "We need to find out, though. More importantly, we need to figure out who that girl is and what she was doing here."

"I'm guessing we need to start with this room." Kreskin was resigned. "We need to open it."

Rob pulled out a crowbar. "I'm on it. Stand back."

"WHAT DO YOU KNOW ABOUT MILDRED?" Maddie asked as she

dunked her teabag in the hot water. "I mean ... you guys were the same age, right?"

Maude made an exaggerated face. "I'll have you know that Mildred was three years older than me. She was old. I'm not old."

Maddie merely nodded. "Right. I'm sorry. I didn't mean to offend you."

"She didn't hang around with us much," Maude admitted, sobering. "She was kind of a loner."

"She was more than a loner," Rosemary countered. "She was actually a very unfriendly person, to the point where she told us she thought we were silly and should focus on something other than making Harriet a very unhappy woman."

"As if that's not important," Maude scoffed. "Making Harriet lose her marbles is definitely more interesting than anything Mildred was doing."

"What do you know about her family, though?" Maddie persisted. "I mean ... did she have children?"

"Well, that's a good question." Maude scratched the top of her head. "I think she might've had a son. I need to give it some thought, though. You have to understand, she's been alone in that house for a really long time. Her husband died a good twenty years ago. I didn't pay her much attention because she didn't like me."

"I believe her exact comment is that you were silly," Rosemary offered helpfully. "You didn't like that at all."

"I still don't like it," Maude said pointedly, cajoling a small smile out of Maddie. "Don't forget that. I'm definitely not silly."

Rosemary sobered. "No. You're not."

"I don't understand how Mildred could have a child in that house and no one ever noticed," Maddie persisted. "How is that even possible?"

Maude shrugged. "I don't know. She was unlikable so nobody ever stopped in. Even the Meals on Wheels people said she was too mean to feed. I think they were hoping she would starve to death."

Maddie pinned her grandmother with a hard look. "That is mean and nasty and I don't like it. Mildred is dead. They found her body."

"And that's a tragedy," Maude fired back. "No one deserves to die that way. The thing is, are you still going to be feeling sorry for her if you find out she did something to that kid you've already attached yourself to?"

Maddie balked. "I'm not attached to her."

"You are. I see it on your face. You're angry at Nick for helping that woman drag her away and your dreams are going to be a dark place until you figure out a way to help. I know you, Maddie."

Unfortunately, Maddie recognized that was true. Her grandmother knew her better than almost anyone. Nick was the lone exception. "I understand Nick had a job to do. I'm not angry at him." Maddie said the words, but she wasn't sure if she meant them. "He did what he had to do."

"Keep saying that over and over and maybe you'll believe it by the time he gets home." Maude slowly got to her feet and rapped on the table to get Joni's attention. "We should get going. We have a schedule to keep." Her eyes were serious when she turned back to Maddie. "I'll ask around tonight, see what everyone knows about Mildred. Just because I didn't care to be friendly with her, that doesn't mean everyone else felt the same."

Maddie nodded in thanks. "Great. That's good."

"As for you, I think you need to calm yourself before Nick gets home. You're going to be upset if you fight. You know that."

Maddie *did* know that. "I'm going to take a bath and relax. I promise."

"Good girl. Keep me updated if you find any good information."

"You'll be my first call."

NICK FOUND MADDIE curled up in the window-seat bed Olivia fashioned for them when they were children when he got home. It was almost midnight and he was exhausted.

He wanted a shower. What he wanted more than that was Maddie. The sight of her angelic face as she slumbered soothed some of his frayed nerves.

He left her long enough to clean up, standing underneath the pounding water until he felt human again. Maddie was awake when he returned to the main floor, her eyes glittering under the limited light.

"I'm sorry, Mad." Nick lifted the blanket and climbed into the window seat with her, ignoring the look she gave him when he nudged her over. "I didn't mean to wake you."

"It's fine. I wasn't really asleep."

Maddie's response was stiff, but Nick ignored it, sliding his arm under her waist and tugging until her head landed on his chest. If she wanted to be angry, that was her right. Nick wasn't about to make it easy on her, though.

"I'm pretty sure you were asleep," Nick countered. "You were snoring and drooling when I came in."

"I don't snore!"

"At least you're owning up to the drooling. That's progress."

Maddie glowered at him, causing Nick to smile. "I don't drool either."

"Has anyone ever told you how cute you are when you pretend to be angry?" Nick asked, hoping his natural charm would erode her fury. "I think you could be the cutest angry woman ever."

Maddie rolled her eyes. "I know what you're trying to do."

"Love you?"

"Ugh. I hate it when you do that. It makes it impossible to stay mad."

"That's what I was going for." Nick tucked her in tight at his side, resting his cheek against her forehead as he wrapped his arms around her. "I know you're upset about what happened earlier. I can't change that. I did what I thought was right."

"I know. I'm not angry. Er, well, not really angry."

"So, basically you're saying you're not Hulk angry, right?"

"Ugh." Maddie lightly slapped his chest. "Her face is going to haunt me, Nicky."

"I know, love. I'm so sorry." He kissed her forehead. "She had to go with the people who could help her, though. We're not those people. I'm sorry."

"What you're saying makes sense in my head. My heart still hurts, though."

"I know. That's because you're the sweetest woman in the world."

"You don't need to keep saying things like that. I'm no longer angry with you."

"Good to know."

They lapsed into comfortable silence for a moment. Nick was eager for Maddie to get some sleep. Heck, he was eager to join her. They had something to discuss first, though.

"Mad, I don't really want to get into this now – mostly because I'm not sure what it all means – but that girl was locked in the basement room," Nick said quietly. "Mildred had a padlock on the outside. She couldn't have gotten out no matter what."

Maddie's heart skipped a beat. "What does that mean?"

"I don't know."

"Who is she?"

"I don't know." Nick clasped Maddie tighter, thankful for her warmth. "The room was neat and tidy, not filthy or anything. There was a bed, a nightstand, and some books. There was a tray so it looked as if Mildred was feeding her."

"She was still locked in."

"I know. I'm going to get answers, Mad. There's nothing more I can do tonight, though. I just thought you should know."

"Well, now I know." Maddie brushed a quick kiss against Nick's strong jaw. "You're going to have nightmares because of it, aren't you?"

"I hope not."

"I think I might, too."

Nick hated the resignation in her voice. "How about we focus on each other and do our best to keep out the nightmares?"

That was easier said than done, Maddie knew, but she was eager to give it a try. "Sure. Tell me how cute I am when I'm angry again. I think that will help."

Nick chuckled as he gave in to his fatigue. "You're the absolute prettiest woman in the world. All other women pale compared to you."

"That's a good start."

"I thought so."

5. FIVE

Nick groaned as he stretched the next morning, his back making horrific cracking noises as he extended his lanky frame and rolled.

"Oh, man. I think I'm officially getting too old to sleep in the window seat."

Maddie, rubbing sleep from her eyes, made a sympathetic sound as she patted his arm.

"I'm serious," Nick grumbled. "I can't stretch out in this thing. It's fine for a nap or one of our marathon book-reading sessions. Sleep should be done in our bed, though."

"All you had to do was mention it." Maddie found her voice, although it was low and gravelly. She was often a slow-starter in the morning. "I didn't think about it. I'm sorry."

Nick tucked a strand of hair behind her ear and smiled. "I got to sleep with you. I guess it was worth it."

"Ha, ha." Maddie poked his side. "You need to get up."

Nick's eyes lit with wicked intent. "That's exactly what I was thinking. Let's go upstairs and spend a little bit of time getting reacquainted with our bed."

Maddie wasn't about to fall for that. "I meant that you need to get up and call the CPS lady. What was her name again?"

"Sharon."

"Yeah. Call her and make sure that girl is okay. I need to know."

Nick ran his tongue over his teeth as he regarded her. He wasn't eager to see her reaction when he said what he had to say, but he understood it had to be done. "Mad, maybe you should take a step back from this."

"No."

"But ... I hate seeing you upset and no matter what happens with that girl you're going to be upset."

"I said no." Maddie refused to back down. "I'm involved. I know you don't want me to get invested, but it's too late. I became invested the minute I helped that girl from the basement. You know it as well as I do. I can't go back."

Nick rubbed his hand over the top of his hair. "I know. I just ... I hate it when you get riled up."

"I thought you wanted to go upstairs just so you could rile me up."

Nick's lips curved. "There's riling and there's riling."

"I'll participate in whatever form you want if you call." Maddie was serious. "Please. For me."

Nick could do nothing but acquiesce. "Okay, but then we're definitely going upstairs to spend quality time with our bed ... and probably the shower, too. I think they miss us."

"I can live with that."

"Fine." Nick propped himself on his elbow. "Where is my phone?"

"YOU LOOK BETTER THIS morning than you did last night," Maude announced as she danced behind the counter while waiting for the coffee to finish brewing. Maddie and Nick were upstairs so long they had no idea Maude had even returned. "Did you guys make up?"

"We weren't fighting," Maddie said as she edged around Maude and headed toward the refrigerator. "We were tense because of other things, not because we were fighting."

Maude snorted. "Whatever. I saw the look on your face. You were spoiling for a fight."

"She *was* spoiling for a fight," Nick agreed. "I talked her out of it, though."

"And how did you do that?"

"I have a natural ability to make women fall at my feet." Nick winked at Maddie, enjoying the way her cheeks flushed with a mixture of pleasure and embarrassment. "They can't help themselves. I'm the drug they just can't stop sniffing."

Maude rolled her eyes. "I bet that sounded cooler in your head than it did coming out."

"Totally," Nick agreed, sitting at the table as Maddie began gathering breakfast ingredients. "By the way, I checked in with the station this morning and it's the funniest thing. Someone toilet-papered Harriet Proctor's yard last night. I don't know about you, but I'm shocked that anyone would go after that poor woman."

To her credit, Maude didn't show a hint of reaction. "That's terrible. I hope they find who did it."

"Oh, and also, the big package of toilet paper I bought the other day disappeared out of our bathroom cabinet," Nick added. "There's only one roll left."

"Maybe you used more than you realized," Maude suggested.

"I guess that must be it."

Maddie glanced between her grandmother and Nick, her lips curving before grabbing two pans from the cupboard and placing them on the stove. "Nick called the woman from Child Protective Services this morning. The girl I found is doing better, although she's still not talking."

Maude took the conversational shift in stride. "That's good. I bet that makes you feel better, huh?"

"It makes me feel somewhat better," Maddie clarified. "I still want to see her."

"Is that possible?" Maude turned to Nick. "I mean ... is she allowed to see her?"

"I would've thought not given everything that's going on, but when I called the social worker she said it didn't sound like a bad idea."

"Huh."

"Of course, she said that after Maddie grabbed the phone from my hand and insisted on seeing the girl," Nick added. "Sharon argued at first but then gave in. Apparently I'm not the only one who can't resist Maddie's charms."

"Oh, don't kid yourself." Maddie upended a full bag of pre-chopped hash browns into a skillet. "She agreed because of you. She thinks you're hot and she's hopeful you'll be with me for the visit."

"I think you're exaggerating."

"And I think she went all breathless when she heard your voice," Maddie countered. "She was all 'Detective Winters, I'm so glad to hear from you.'" Maddie adopted a high-pitched giggle. "She definitely cares more about you than me. I don't care, though, because she cleared the way for me to visit ... well, the girl." Maddie made a face. "We need something to call her besides 'the girl.' That seems rude."

"Hopefully Sharon will be able to get a name out of her," Nick said. "There were a lot of books in her room, and they were more middle-grade books – like Harry Potter and *The Hunger Games* – so I think it's fair to say she can read. If she can read, she can communicate, even if she can't speak."

"Hmm. I didn't think of that." Maddie tapped her bottom lip. "I'm going to take Christy shopping before we head over there. I'll get things like notebooks and pens and some books for her."

"You're going shopping?" Nick's eyebrows migrated up his forehead. "When did you decide that?"

"When you were shaving. I already texted Christy. We're picking up some clothes and other items, too."

"But ... don't you think you're going a little overboard?"

"No." Maddie sprayed the second pan with oil and reached for the eggs. "How many eggs does everyone want?"

"Two," Maude answered automatically, shooting Nick a warning look when he opened his mouth. She could tell he was about to argue further and Maude recognized it was a bad idea. "Don't," she said, keeping her voice low. "You can't talk her out of this. Your best option is to show her support if you don't want her to dig her heels in."

Nick didn't often take advice from Maude because ... well, because she was nutty. He loved her but didn't think of her as a fountain of relationship advice. Still, this time at least, he knew she was probably right.

"Three eggs," Nick called out, flashing a smile when Maddie snagged his gaze. "I'm starving. For some reason I worked up an appetite this morning."

Maddie smirked. "I did, too. I think I'm going to have three eggs as well."

"Good. I like it when we're on the same page."

"Me, too."

"WHAT DO YOU THINK ABOUT THIS?"

Christy Ford, her red hair spilling over her shoulders in a series of rambunctious curls, held up a pink shirt that made Maddie cringe.

"I don't know about that," Maddie hedged, searching her mind for a way to shoot down the shirt without agitating her friend. "The color is a bit much."

"It's pink. Pink is a happy color."

Maddie had never really considered the color pink anything but an annoying color. "I think she's more of a purple person." Maddie held up a simple lavender T-shirt for emphasis. "I think this looks more like her."

Christy furrowed her brow as she studied the garment in question. "I'm confused. I thought you said she was a kid."

"She is."

"That's an adult size small, though," Christy pointed out. "Is she a kid or a teenager?"

Maddie chewed on her bottom lip as she debated how to answer. "I don't know," she admitted finally. "I thought she was about eleven or so ... maybe thirteen ... but Nick thinks she's at least fifteen."

Christy widened her eyes. "That's a big discrepancy."

"I know." Maddie's stomach twisted. "She was tiny and really pale. I honestly don't know how old she is. I'm kind of eyeing the clothing."

"Then we'll go with your gut." Christy was matter of fact. "It hasn't steered you wrong before. What do you want to get her?"

"I'm thinking a couple of pairs of pants and some tops. Some pajamas wouldn't hurt. Some slippers. Then I want to get her comfort items, like coloring books and regular books. Maybe a stuffed animal or something."

"If she's a teenager, she might take the stuffed animal as an insult."

"I don't think so. You didn't see her. She clung to me like ... she didn't have anything else in the world to hold on to. I think a stuffed animal will be good for her."

Christy's expression softened. "Okay. That doesn't sound terrible. Let's pick the clothes first."

Maddie and Christy busied themselves selecting a variety of things, including track pants, jeans, shirts, a hoodie, socks, and underwear. Then they moved to the toiletries aisle and picked out several things they thought she might need before heading to the book aisle.

"It's a good thing adult coloring books are still in fashion," Christy noted. "They have Harry Potter. Didn't you say she liked Harry Potter?"

Maddie automatically nodded as she studied the books. "Nick said he saw *The Hunger Games* and Harry Potter books." She selected a boxed-set trilogy. "This is *Divergent*. I think that's supposed to be like *The Hunger Games*."

Christy shrugged. "You've got me. I don't read that stuff. I prefer an old-fashioned bodice ripper with lots of sex."

"You would." Maddie shoved the books in the cart. "I need to grab something else for her. I don't want to get something that skews too young, though, because I want her to feel challenged."

"Well, I've picked out three coloring books," Christy supplied. "Do you want crayons or colored pencils?"

"Both. Get markers, too."

"How much money are you planning to spend here, Maddie?"

"However much it takes." Maddie was firm as she grabbed another book and looked at the back cover. "Teenagers like fantasy books, right?"

"I would think so." Christy leaned on the handle of the cart as she regarded her friend. "Do you want to tell me why you're so manic about this?"

"I'm not manic." Maddie evaded Christy's gaze. "I don't understand why you think I'm acting manic."

"Because you are." Christy kept her voice easy and calm. "I get that it must have shaken you to see her, but you got her out. That's the important thing."

"I didn't even know she was a kid until I had her out," Maddie admitted. "When I saw the ghost ... well, I didn't recognize her. I knew it wasn't Mildred, though. I thought maybe Mildred was in the basement."

"Oh, that makes sense."

"She was light, though. Like ... way too light. Once I had my hands on her I realized she was frail. She looked so lost all I wanted was to protect her. When Nick told me the room was locked from the outside, I swear I wanted to hurt someone. I don't consider myself a violent person and yet I think I would've killed Mildred myself right then and there."

"You don't know that Mildred is responsible," Christy cautioned. "Right now, we have no idea what was going on in that house."

"I guess that's fair. I'm still angry, though."

"Which is why we're shopping I guess, huh?" Christy's smile turned into a grimace as she moved her hand to her stomach. She was generally full of smiles, but she seemed a bit more agitated than normal today.

"It is," Maddie agreed, concern washing over her. "Are you okay?"

"I'm fine." Christy waved off the question. "John and I ordered spring rolls from the Chinese place last night and I think they were bad. I've been feeling off ever since."

Maddie was instantly sympathetic. "Do you think you have food poisoning?"

"I don't know. It's a possibility." Eager to turn the conversation away from her digestive problems, Christy focused on the coloring books. "Maybe, if you're going all out and want to keep her mind occupied, it might not be such a bad idea to grab a few of those puzzle books. That might entertain her."

"Oh, that's a good idea." Maddie scampered to the other side of the aisle and perused the selection, grabbing three and a package of gel pens on display at the bottom of the rack before turning back to the cart. When she did, she found Christy bent over completely and wiping sweat from her brow. "Are you going to be sick? Should we find the bathroom?"

Christy scowled at the suggestion. "I am not going to be sick. I don't get sick."

"You look sick. You're all ... sweaty. Maybe you have the flu or something."

"I don't get sick," Christy repeated.

"You just said you might have food poisoning."

"Yes, but that doesn't mean I'm going to get sick," Christy countered, tapping the side of her head rather viciously. "It's mind power, you see. If you don't believe you can get sick, you won't get sick."

Maddie was understandably dubious. "Is this like when we went to the bar a couple of weeks ago and you said you could will yourself into not getting a hangover and then you yelled at me the next day when I suggested we take a walk because you had the world's worst hangover?"

Christy scowled. "This is nothing like that."

"Good to know."

"I don't get sick, though." Christy was firm as she wiped her brow. "Seriously. I feel as if I'm having a hot flash. What's the earliest someone can go into menopause?"

The question triggered something in Maddie's brain. "Wait ... you're not pregnant, are you?"

Christy's mouth dropped open. "How can you even ask that?"

"That wasn't a denial," Maddie pointed out. "As for how I can ask it, you and John have been together for a few months and if the stories he tells Nick are true you've been very ... um, active ... during that time."

"Oh, my ... I'm going to kill him." Christy made a disgusted face. "I'm going to totally kill him ... with pain."

Since Maddie had known John since she was a small child – he was Nick's older brother, after all – she found herself caught up in the idea of Christy being pregnant. "I think it would be so much fun if you were pregnant," Maddie enthused. "I mean ... how much fun would a baby be? We could dress her up and get one of those jogging strollers so you can have an easy time getting in shape after the birth."

The look Christy shot Maddie promised mayhem. "I am not pregnant. Stop saying that."

"But you're sick to your stomach." Maddie adopted a pragmatic tone. "That could be morning sickness."

"It's almost eleven. That's not really morning."

Maddie ignored the argument. "You said you felt like you were having a hot flash. That could mean your hormones are out of whack, which totally happens when you're pregnant."

"Ugh." Christy straightened and glared. "I can't believe you're still going on like this. I am not pregnant."

"How do you know?"

"Because I'm on the pill."

"The pill isn't always a hundred percent effective," Maddie argued. "Sometimes the pill fails."

"Not when you take it correctly." Christy refused to back down. "I am not pregnant and if I hear that rumor around town I'm going to know exactly who started it."

Maddie had the grace to be abashed. "I'm sorry." She held up her hands in capitulation. "I didn't mean to upset you."

"It's fine." Christy was cranky, but she knew it was impossible to stay mad at Maddie over the long haul. "Let's finish shopping and then get out of here. I want to meet this girl now that you've talked about her so much."

"Good idea." Maddie tilted her head to the side and regarded Christy with keen interest. "Do you want a girl? I think you should have a girl. She would be so much more fun to dress up."

Christy let loose a mock scream as she turned on her heel. "I hate you right now."

"I definitely think you should have a girl," Maddie added. "What are you going to name her?"

6. SIX

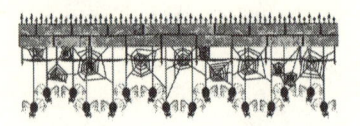

The children's home was located in a rural area just outside of Traverse City. Since Maddie and Christy opted to shop at a nearby Target, it didn't take them long to reach the home once they were finished and loaded.

The trunk of Christy's car was overflowing when they opened it and Maddie opted to take as many bags as possible so Christy wouldn't be weighed down.

"I can take more," Christy offered, puzzled by Maddie's insistence on carrying the bulk of the items. "You don't have to take everything."

"I'm fine." Maddie flashed a bright smile. "I don't want you to carry too much. It might hurt the baby."

Christy's lips turned down. "I don't think you're funny. Not even a little."

Maddie wasn't bothered by her friend's tone. She was used to Christy's crabby attitude. "Do you have names picked out? I think you should go with Maddie for a little girl and Parker for a boy."

Christy made an exaggerated face. "You're so ... obnoxious. I am not pregnant."

Now that she'd started the game, Maddie refused to back down. "Think how great it would be if you were."

"I'm not pregnant," Christy repeated, her anger on full display.

"Stop saying that. Besides, I would never name a kid of mine Parker. I'm not happy with you right now either so Maddie is out of the question as well."

"You'll get over it." Maddie's smile stayed in place until she walked through the front door and pulled up short. She didn't know what she was expecting, but the drab gray walls and depressing atmosphere were pretty far from appealing. "This can't be right."

"Ugh. Look at this place." Christy's disdain was evident. "No one should have to live here."

"It needs some refurbishing," Sharon agreed, popping out of a side office and causing both women to jolt. "We do the best we can with the funds we're allocated. We opt to spend the money on the children rather than new paint."

Maddie's cheeks burned under the woman's scrutiny. "We didn't mean anything by it."

"We didn't," Christy agreed. "It's just so ... gray."

"Yes, well, I wouldn't mind a color spruce myself, but I have other things to deal with first." Sharon extended a hand and then pulled back slightly when she realized Maddie's hands were full of bags. "We didn't get a chance to meet yesterday. I'm Sharon Lansing."

"Maddie Graves." Maddie was sheepish as she shifted from one foot to the other. "I'm sorry about yesterday, by the way. You probably think I'm an emotional mess after what happened. I just ... I was upset because she was upset."

"I understand that." Sharon was professional if not overly friendly. "I get it. Detective Winters explained that you're the one who found her. We're lucky you did because if you hadn't vented that room there's a good chance the smoke would've overwhelmed her."

"Well, I wasn't thinking that far ahead," Maddie admitted. "I simply saw movement and acted. I honestly thought it might be Mildred until I got her outside. Then I realized she was a child and ... well, I lost my head a bit."

"That's perfectly understandable." Sharon gestured toward a bench placed against a nearby wall. "Sit, please. We need to discuss a few things before I let you see her."

"Sure." Maddie was uncomfortable with the woman's clipped tone. "Is something wrong?"

"Yes and no. The thing is, we have been unable to make any headway with her. She screams when someone enters her room, she slept under the bed instead of in it last night, and she basically sits huddled in a corner and won't let anyone touch her."

The news didn't surprise Maddie, but it did cause her stomach to twist. "Maybe she'll react better to seeing me."

"That's why I agreed to allow your visit," Sharon said. "It's not something we regularly do, but I'm desperate enough to skew from the rules. If the girl – and we don't have a name – has somehow bonded with you then we'd like to use that as a tool to get her to communicate.

"Also, you have to understand, we've been unable to give her even a cursory examination because she doesn't want anyone to touch her," she continued. "She hasn't bathed or brushed her teeth. She refuses to change out of the nightgown she was in when you found her. We're at the point where we might have to sedate her if we want to examine her."

"Oh, don't do that." Maddie was crushed at the thought. "Let me try. I can't guarantee that it will work, but it couldn't possibly hurt to let me try."

"That's the plan." Sharon got to her feet. "I see you went all out shopping for her."

"Just a few things." Maddie hated feeling defensive, but Sharon's tone put her on edge. "I can take it back but ... I really would rather not."

"Well ... ."

"There's nothing in here that can hurt anyone," Christy offered helpfully. "If Maddie takes it in there she might be so excited by the new things that it will loosen her lips. I don't see what the big deal is."

"There are other children in this home," Sharon argued. "If this girl gets everything it might cause an uproar."

"Well, you won't know until it happens." Christy was firm. She wasn't used to people arguing with her and was in no mood to start allowing it today. "Let's just see if Maddie can get through to her."

"Fine."

CHRISTY AGREED TO REMAIN in the hallway with Sharon and allowed Maddie to enter the girl's room alone. No one wanted to overwhelm her and there was an observation window built right into the wall.

Maddie knocked before entering, plastering a bright smile on her face, and it took her a moment to scan the room. The girl was huddled in the corner until she saw Maddie. Then, suddenly, she was on her feet and throwing herself at the surprised blonde.

"Hello." Maddie's voice was soft, like music, and her fingers were gentle as she combed them through the girl's hair. "I'm so glad to see you. I'm sorry I couldn't come sooner but ... well, I'm here now."

Maddie lowered herself to the ground so she was on the same level with the girl, who refused to move from Maddie's side and instead stared into her blue eyes as if trying to communicate telepathically. Her expression was so earnest Maddie thought she might burst into tears. Since she was afraid that would terrify her new friend, Maddie instead forced herself to remain upbeat.

"Still not talking, huh?"

The girl shook her head, boosting Maddie's hopes that she could understand but simply didn't want to talk.

"Well, that's okay." Maddie meant it. "I bought some things for you at the store." She gestured toward the bags she left by the door. "I was thinking that we could get you cleaned up and in some new clothes – maybe spend some time together looking at your new books and stuff – and then maybe you'll feel like talking after that. How does that sound?"

The girl bit her lip and stared hard into Maddie's eyes.

"It's okay," Maddie offered. "You don't have to answer right now. We'll take it one step at a time."

The girl continued to stare and she didn't appear afraid of Maddie.

"We're going to start with a bath." Maddie was firm as she moved to stand. "Don't worry. I'm going to be with you the entire time. You smell like smoke, though, and we can barely see that pretty face under all the grime."

Maddie looked to the window, knowing Sharon was on the other side, for help. "Where is the nearest bathroom?"

NICK READ THE TEXT from Christy three times before placing his cell phone on his desk and scowling. He leaned back in his desk chair and stretched – his back was still giving him issues from the position he'd slept in the previous night – and he was eager to work out all the kinks.

"Who was that?" Kreskin asked, dropping off a cup of coffee on the corner of Nick's desk before sliding into his chair.

"Christy."

"Is something wrong with Maddie?" Kreskin was well aware that Nick was a bit obsessive when it came to his fiancée's safety. Instinctively he knew that if Maddie were in real trouble Nick would already be gone. Given Maddie's mood the previous evening, though, Kreskin was convinced that Nick's issues with Maddie might be of the emotional sort. "She's okay, isn't she?"

"Physically she's fine," Nick replied. "Emotionally she makes me want to ... ." He broke off and mimed choking an invisible person, causing Kreskin to smile.

"Welcome to marriage, son."

"We're not married yet."

"Close enough." Kreskin leaned back in his chair and sipped his coffee. "Do you want to tell me what's bothering you?"

"There are so many things bothering me I don't know where to start."

"How about with what Christy messaged you?"

"Oh, *that*." Nick rolled his neck until it cracked. "She's with Maddie at the children's home in Traverse City."

"Oh." Realization dawned on Kreskin as amusement took over. "So, your plan to completely remove Maddie from the situation is going well, huh?"

"Don't push me," Nick warned, extending a finger. "It's not funny."

"It's a little funny."

"No."

"Son, you have got to stop letting things like this trip you up." Kreskin adopted a pragmatic tone. "Maddie is her own person. She has feelings and beliefs. She's a good person and that means she's going to occasionally put herself on the line. You didn't really think she was going to just let this go, did you?"

"I kind of hoped she would."

"Well, then you were dreaming." Kreskin saw no reason to coddle his partner. "Has she seen the girl? Has she learned anything?"

"All Christy said was that Maddie and the girl have been spending a lot of time together," Nick replied. "She's not talking yet. Maddie gave her a bath and is now brushing and braiding her hair. That's what the text said anyway."

"It sounds like Maddie is doing the exact right thing to get that girl to open up," Kreskin noted. "I don't know how you can be angry about that."

"Because I think we both know that something horrible happened in Mildred's house," Nick supplied. "I'm going to guess that means something horrible happened to that girl. When Maddie knows the truth, it's going to crush her."

"Don't you think Maddie already suspects?"

"Yes. Knowing and suspecting are different things, though."

"They certainly are," Kreskin agreed. "You have to let Maddie do what feels natural to her, though. You can't control her."

"I don't want to control her. I ... who said I wanted to control her?"

Kreskin had to bite back a laugh at Nick's annoyed response. "Fine. That wasn't the right word. You want to protect her, not control her."

"Is that so bad?"

"No, but you can't protect her when she doesn't want to be protected," Kreskin pointed out. "Right now, she wants to do the saving. I think you're going to have to let her."

"Yeah." Nick rubbed his forehead. "I can't do anything about it anyway. What I can tell you is that I've been trying to dig into Mildred's past and all I keep coming up with are dead ends. It's almost as if she wasn't who she said she was."

Kreskin shoved worry for his partner's love life out of his mind and, interest piqued, leaned forward. "What do you mean?"

"There's nothing. I can't find a trail to follow."

"That can't be right."

"And yet it is."

"Well, let's dig deeper."

"Go for it. Hopefully you will have better luck than me."

"SHE'S GOOD WITH HER."

Sharon couldn't help but be impressed as she watched Maddie braid the girl's hair, all the while keeping up a running conversation that the child showed very little interest in. She was far more entranced by the coloring books and artistic supplies Maddie brought.

"Who? Maddie?" Christy nodded as she watched. She was feeling markedly better and was hopeful she'd managed to sidestep a bout of food poisoning after all. "She's always had a way about her. People just sort of gravitate to her."

"It's probably the way she looks." Sharon did her best not to sound bitter but failed, causing Christy to smirk.

"Let me guess, you caught sight of Nick first yesterday and your hormones kicked into overdrive," Christy noted. "Then you realized he was with Maddie and all hope fled. I get it but ... you really need to get over it."

Sharon balked. "I have no idea what you're talking about. I mean

... really. I don't even know the man. Yesterday was the first time we met."

"That doesn't mean he's not hotter than most male models, which makes it even more difficult because he's straight and you just want to take a big bite out of that firm rear end of his."

Sharon's mouth dropped open. "I ... you ... ."

"Don't worry about it." Christy waved off the woman's obvious discomfort with a dismissive hand gesture. "Nick Winters has left a trail of broken hearts in his wake. You're hardly the first."

"Oh, well, I don't think my heart is broken."

"But you were attracted to him, weren't you?"

Sharon shrugged, clearly uncomfortable. "He's an attractive man."

"He is, and he made the rounds for ten years, crushing women left and right as he tried to make sense of his life."

"I don't understand what that means."

"It's a long story," Christy said. "I'll make it short. Nick and Maddie loved each other in high school but were too afraid to admit it. She left to become a nurse. He stayed and became a cop. For ten years they pined for one another.

"After her mother died, Maddie came home," she continued. "They took one look at one another and their worlds went sideways. They've been joined at the hip ever since."

"That was a fascinating story," Sharon drawled. "Why on earth did you tell it to me?"

"So you'll understand that it's nothing personal. Nick didn't look past you. It's just ... all he can see is Maddie. I never believed in destiny or soul mates until I saw them together. Now I believe that maybe that thing about there being one person for everybody is true. Those two are definitely soul mates."

"I'm not jealous of her," Sharon said hurriedly. "I simply thought he was hot."

"It's fine." Christy was blasé. "Maddie has a way with people. That's why she'll be good for that girl." She turned her eyes back to the window, to where Maddie was bent over and coloring with her young charge. "You know how some people are magical? Maddie is one of those people."

"She clearly seems to be doing well with our guest," Sharon noted. "The thing is ... I don't know what to do if she won't talk. We don't have a name. Our best guess is that she's about fifteen."

Christy was horrified. "Truly? She's so small."

"She is, but even though she's thin she's not malnourished," Sharon said. "She might have some health issues, but we need to get her to a doctor to be sure. Hopefully Maddie will be able to calm her."

"She already has," Christy noted. "In fact ... ." She broke off and leaned closer to the window, her attention completely drawn to the girl's hands. They were moving, and in a way Christy recognized as something beyond simple gestures. "Look at that."

"What?" Sharon followed Christy's finger with her eyes. "I ... is she doing sign language?"

"I can't be certain, but it sure looks that way to me," Christy replied. "I mean ... all I ever learned was the alphabet. She looks as if she's trying to have a conversation with Maddie."

"Do you think Maddie realizes that?"

"There's one way to find out." Christy reached for the door handle, pausing before pushing inside. "Can you get someone who knows sign language here?"

Sharon nodded without hesitation. "Absolutely. I'll place a call right now."

"Good. I think we're about to have a breakthrough or something. Maddie needs to know, though. I think she knows the same alphabet I do. We learned it at the same Girl Scouts camp when we were kids."

"I'll be right back." Sharon's level of excitement grew. "I think we're actually going to be able to help this girl now. I can't tell you how relieved I am."

"That makes two of us."

7. SEVEN

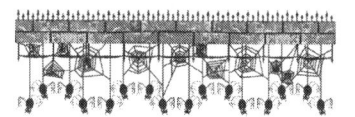

Nick and Kreskin headed to the medical examiner's office one town over when they realized they were getting nowhere trying to track Mildred's family tree. Nick's frustration at the effort was obvious when they landed in the parking lot.

"I don't get it. I mean ... I can see how things like that would slip through the cracks in olden times."

"Like when I was young?" Kreskin teased.

Nick refused to rise to the bait. "You know what I mean. This is the computer age. All this stuff should be trackable."

"I don't disagree with you." Kreskin sobered. "The thing is, Mildred was older. Computers weren't a thing when she was born. I think some of that information fell through the cracks. Going forward things like this won't happen. Looking back, though, well ... we've got our hands full."

"There has to be a record of that girl's birth," Nick complained. "She didn't just hatch out of an egg and miraculously appear in Mildred's basement."

"No, she didn't." Kreskin held open the door so Nick didn't have to break his stride while entering the medical examiner's office. "We'll figure out who she is. I thought you said Christy sent a text that they were getting somewhere."

"They did, but she didn't get into specifics. She said she was too busy."

"So, maybe she is too busy," Kreskin suggested. "You should have faith in Maddie. She's come through a number of times before. This time probably won't be any different."

Nick balked. "I do have faith in Maddie. I'm the one who believes she can do anything."

"Then what are you afraid of?"

Nick worked his jaw. They both knew what he was really afraid of. It was an ugly thought he didn't want to give voice to.

"That's what I thought," Kreskin said after a beat, refusing to back down. "We can only take this one step at a time. This is the first step."

Nick knew he was right and yet he couldn't shake his worry about Maddie. "I hope we can find answers on this sooner rather than later."

"That really would be a nice change of pace, wouldn't it?"

PATTY FOSTER WAS IN her forties and boasted a round and pleasing face. She smiled at Christy and Sharon as she followed them to the observation room, seemingly unbothered by the story they shared upon her arrival.

"She's definitely using sign language," Patty said after a beat, furrowing her brow. "Who is the woman with her?"

"Maddie Graves," Christy answered automatically. "She found the girl in a basement during a fire in Blackstone Bay."

"The girl has bonded to her," Sharon added. "She won't interact with anyone else."

"Well, she's trying to communicate with her now," Patty noted, her eyes intent. "She's trying to tell a story I think, although she's getting frustrated that Maddie doesn't understand. Speaking of that ... I recognize the name. I can't remember where I recognize the name from, though."

Christy was confused. "Which name?"

"Maddie Graves."

"Oh, it's really Madeline Graves," Christy offered. "Um ... she's been in the news a few times since she got back. Er, I mean, she lived here and then Detroit and came back about a year ago."

"She has?" Sharon widened her eyes. "Why has she made the news?"

"Um ... she's had a few things happen to her." Christy chose her words carefully. "Like that fake psychic in Blackstone Bay a few months ago. Maddie is the one who took him down." Christy left out the part where Maddie saved her in the process. "She's also found a few missing people, including that baby who was stolen by the aunt."

"Oh, I remember those stories." Sharon's face brightened considerably. "She's famous."

"She's also the one who is responsible for putting Todd Winthrop behind bars," Patty supplied, her expression unreadable. "His trial is coming up soon, in fact. She was on the news report I saw the other day. That's why I recognized her."

Christy swallowed hard, searching the woman's face for clues. "Did you know Todd?"

Patty bobbed her head. "I did."

"I did, too," Christy acknowledged. "We went to high school together. He tried to kill Maddie that night at the lake. Whatever he says, however he denies it, she almost died."

Patty blinked several times, her expression immovable. "Are you under the impression that I'm standing up for Todd?"

Christy held her hands palms out and shrugged. "I don't know. Todd was known for charming people. Maddie barely survived that night, though, so I don't want to hear about how Todd has been framed or that other nonsense he's been spouting."

"The world would be a better place if Todd didn't survive that night," Patty supplied. "Don't worry. I'm not a fan. Well, I am, but I'm a fan of what she did. She stopped him from killing."

"She did," Christy agreed.

"She almost died in the process," Patty added.

"She did." Christy's memory went back to the night in question. "Nick was there. He swam out in the cold water. It should've killed both of them, but he refused to let her go. He actually performed CPR and got her back."

"And I thought he was hot before I heard this story," Sharon muttered, eliciting a legitimate smile from Christy.

"They've pretty much been inseparable from that moment on," Christy said, smiling at the memory. "Well, actually, they fought it for a good two weeks after that, but everyone knew it was inevitable."

"Yes, well, inevitable or not, they did everyone in the area a great service by getting Todd off the street," Patty said. "He went out with a friend of mine. He didn't kill her or anything, which is a relief, but he was a jerk and thinking what he could've done to her sends chills down my spine."

"I think it does that for all of us," Christy said. "Are you going to try and talk to the girl?"

Patty nodded. "Yes. I want Maddie to stay in there, though. I think she'll be a calming presence."

"Let's do it," Sharon said. "The faster we know who that girl is, the faster we'll be able to figure out where she belongs."

"SHE DIDN'T DIE of smoke inhalation." The assistant medical examiner, Jason Hamilton, munched on a sandwich as he related the details of Mildred Wilkins' death to Nick and Kreskin. "She was strangled."

Nick scratched his cheek as he tried to keep his discomfort in check. It wasn't the death that bothered him so much – or Mildred's corpse on the gurney – but the fact that Hamilton could eat while standing over her that gave him pause. "Um ... how do you know that?"

"Her windpipe was crushed." Hamilton talked with his mouth full of corned beef and Swiss. "That didn't happen by accident. It also didn't happen due to a fall."

"Hmm." Kreskin and Nick exchanged a weighted look. "That means someone else was in the house," Kreskin said finally. "Whoever it was must have started the fire."

"I see you guys are ahead of me," Rob said, a folder in his hand as he strolled into the examination room. Nick noted that he purposely kept his gaze from Mildred's body and instead focused on the three men standing close to the counter. His demeanor was calm and easy, but Nick knew Rob was uncomfortable being in the presence of death. "I was trying to track you down when I heard you were here."

"I don't know whether to feel lucky or not." Kreskin accepted the file Rob extended toward him. "What did you find?"

"Whoever started the fire used an accelerant. In this case, it was simple gasoline. It was focused on a spot on the second floor, which is why the fire basically stayed up there. If it had been started on the first floor the house would've completely gone up in flames. That's not what happened."

"So you're saying that we're not dealing with a professional," Nick surmised.

"I'm saying that we're not dealing with a professional *arsonist*," Rob clarified. "If our suspect was a pro, he would've known to start the fire on the first floor and let the flames rise to take out the second. Instead, he started it on the second floor and it didn't have the energy to travel to the first floor so there's a decent chance we might be able to track down some evidence. I have an inspector out there now taking samples."

"That's good." Nick rubbed the back of his neck. "So, Mildred was strangled and someone set the house on fire purposely. The question is, did he know that there was a young girl locked in the basement? I mean, the motive would seem to be revenge for something and taking the kid is revenge-worthy, but why go to all that trouble just to leave the kid behind?"

"Maybe he didn't realize the kid was on the premises," Kreskin supplied. "Maybe he thought Mildred did something to her."

"You keep saying 'he,'" Jason noted. "Couldn't it be a female?"

"Technically yes," Nick replied. "However, the statistics on females committing crimes with fire are actually extremely low."

"He's basically saying that men are attracted to fire more than women," Kreskin explained. "Just like women are attracted to poison more than men. You can't rule out that a woman did this, but odds are it was a man."

"I'm going to add to your odds," Jason said. "Whoever killed Mildred had big hands. I don't know a lot of women who have hands big enough to fit the bill."

"Fingerprints?" Nick asked.

Jason shook his head. "Everything on the body was too rough because of the water. You should know she didn't have smoke in her lungs. I think that means the fire was set after she was already dead."

"That makes sense," Kreskin said. "Someone probably panicked after realizing she was dead and set the fire to cover up for the murder, even assumed the fire would engulf the whole house."

"That still doesn't explain who the kid is or why she was locked in the basement," Nick pointed out.

"No, but I do want to show you what I found fused to her hand," Jason said, placing his sandwich on the counter before moving down to a tray. "I thought this might interest you." He held up a silver key. "It looks to me like it belongs to a padlock, the type that was described on the outside of the basement door you guys broke through."

Kreskin snagged the key and stared at it. "This looks right. We'll have to test it to be sure, but I'm willing to bet this key opened the basement door."

"So what was she doing with it in her hand?" Jason asked. "Was she trying to help the kid or hurt her?"

Nick pressed the heel of his hand to his forehead. "That is the question of the day, isn't it?"

PATTY HAD ONE OF THOSE faces that Maddie found instantly trustworthy. Even though she was determined to keep the girl safe and comfortable, Maddie found herself watching Patty for instructional tidbits as the sign language expert got comfortable in the observation room.

"Just keep doing what you're doing," Patty said, her smile friendly but not overbearing as she met the girl's leery expression. "I'm going to repeat everything I say to her and she says back to me out loud so you'll be able to follow along. Since you're more familiar with the situation regarding how she was found, don't be afraid to interject a question if it pops up."

"Okay." Maddie smiled encouragingly at the girl as Patty lifted her fingers and started signing. "Wow. That's impressive."

Patty ignored the compliment and focused on the youngest person in the room. "What is your name?"

The girl stared for a long beat. It was obvious she recognized what Patty was doing with her hands, but she didn't seem keen to answer.

"Go ahead," Maddie prodded, staring into the girl's suspicious eyes. "I need something to call you."

The girl nodded finally and then responded with lightning-quick motions.

"Her name is Angel," Patty translated, her hands busy. "How old are you, Angel? That's a beautiful name, by the way."

Maddie was awestruck as she watched. She wished she could communicate with the girl herself but was so thankful that someone was finally making progress that she refused to feel bitter.

"She's fifteen," Patty supplied. "She's small for fifteen." She didn't sign the second part, but Maddie could tell what she was thinking. "I'm going to ask what she was doing at the house. Hold on."

Maddie watched as Patty signed the question, keeping a strong arm around the girl's shoulders as she stiffened and made a face. "I don't think she likes that question."

"Definitely not," Patty agreed, tilting her head when Angel jutted out her lower lip into a pronounced pout. "Hmm." She started signing again. "Can you hear?"

Angel opened her mouth and then closed it, tilting her head as she watched Patty's fingers. Finally she nodded, causing Maddie to furrow her brow, and started signing furiously.

"She's not completely deaf," Patty volunteered after a beat. "She can hear some things – more in her left ear than her right – but she learned sign language anyway because her mother was told there was a chance she would go completely deaf by the time she was ten. That didn't happen, but she doesn't hear well enough to be comfortable."

"Where is her mother?" Maddie automatically asked.

"Hold on." Patty watched Angel sign with great interest. "Huh. She says she was in the house because she was staying with her grandmother."

Maddie stilled, surprised. "Mildred?"

Patty shrugged. "I'll ask." She signed for a few minutes, the conversation serious as she went back and forth with Angel. When she was done, Patty straightened. "She says Mildred was her grandmother and she was staying with her. I didn't push too hard on the mother, but Angel doesn't want to talk about her. She just says she's not around and then kind of turns belligerent."

"I don't ever remember seeing Mildred with a child," Maddie noted. "At eighty, she's about my grandmother's age. I would think that means any child of hers would've been around my mother's age. I guess that means her child could've moved and left the area before my mother arrived but ... I don't know."

"Well, Angel says Mildred was her grandmother," Patty said. "She's asking about her."

"Oh, well, she's dead." Maddie shifted to get more comfortable. "She died in the fire."

"Should I tell her?"

"I think she already knows," Maddie admitted. "She's not stupid."

"Definitely not," Patty agreed, her hands moving again. "I'm sorry to be the one to tell you this, but your grandmother is dead. There was a fire at the house – I'm pretty sure you know that because you were there – and she died. I'm sorry for your loss."

Angel blinked several times in rapid succession, but her hands remained still. Maddie didn't like the girl's disposition so she immediately tapped her shoulder to get her attention and pointed at her lips so Angel would know to focus.

"I'm sorry this happened to you," Maddie offered haltingly. "It's sad and terrible, but you were locked in that basement. Do you know why?"

Angel shook her head.

"Was your grandmother mean to you?"

Angel shook her head again, this time more vehemently. Then she started signing.

"Not mean," Patty translated. "Afraid. She was afraid that someone would find out I was there. I had to be really quiet and I couldn't go outside. No one could know I was there. It was important that it stayed secret."

The admission caused Maddie's stomach to tilt. Angel might not think her grandmother was mean, but Maddie wasn't certain the girl fully understood the situation. "Well ... we need more information to go on. Your grandmother is gone. Are you sure you don't know what happened to your mother?"

Angel shook her head so hard one of her braids smacked Maddie in the face.

"What about your father?"

For a brief moment, Maddie was convinced she saw something else in Angel's eyes. It looked to be terror. She covered quickly, though.

"She says she doesn't have a father," Patty volunteered.

Maddie didn't believe that for a second. She decided to let it go, though. "Well, then we'll have to figure out a different way to search for information. We're going to need your help, though, Angel."

"What do you want me to do?" Patty translated.

"Well, for starters, we need to know what you remember from yesterday," Maddie said. "We need to know how the fire started. Then we need to know how you got there and if you know anything about any other relatives you have. I think that's the best place to start."

Patty nodded in agreement. "I think that's a good idea, too. Let's talk about yesterday, Angel." Her hands moved quickly. "Start with the time you woke up until the time Maddie pulled you from the basement window. Don't leave anything out."

8. EIGHT

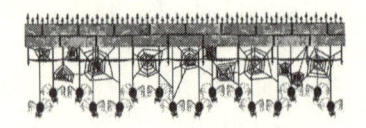

Maddie was reluctant to leave Angel, but Sharon was insistent that the girl get used to her new surroundings without Maddie hovering so she had no choice but to leave once Patty was done questioning her. Patty promised she would stick close to the home and serve as a go-between so Angel would have someone to talk with. Maddie offered a cheery wave and a promise that she would be back before turning grouchy the second she walked through the exit door.

She found her father at the house when she returned. He sat in his car, a dirty look on his face, and when Maddie stopped outside the window she could tell he wasn't in the best of moods. That was fine. She wasn't exactly feeling benevolent at the present moment either. "What happened?"

George mustered a smile for Maddie, but his agitation remained. "I ran into your grandmother when I stopped to see you. Your car was in the driveway so I assumed you were home. She insisted I wait out here rather than in the house in case I tried to steal something from your store."

Maddie didn't know if she should be angry or amused. "Oh, well, that's just how she is. Don't let her get to you."

"I'm pretty sure she's hungover."

"I'm pretty sure you're right," Maddie agreed. "She had a late night terrorizing Harriet Proctor."

"Isn't that how she spends the bulk of her nights?"

"Pretty much." Maddie held open the door as George climbed out of the car. "Not that I'm not happy to see you – because I am – but what are you doing here? We didn't have a lunch date I forgot about or something, did we?"

"No." George's smile turned kind as he regarded his daughter. He'd gone without her so long in his life he still considered it a miracle of sorts that he could just drop in on her when he felt like it. "I saw the news this afternoon and I wanted to check on you."

Maddie furrowed her brow. "The news?"

"About the house down the way." George vaguely gestured. "I heard there was a fire and you pulled a young girl from the house and saved her."

Maddie was dumbfounded. "They put that on the news? I can't believe they used my name. I didn't talk to anyone from the press. They didn't even show up until I was leaving."

George chuckled, genuinely amused. "They didn't say your name. They had one shot of you from a great distance away. You were standing with Nick and looked upset. Then you took off and left him behind, making me think he was upset."

"Oh." Maddie was marginally placated. "He wasn't all that upset."

"He looked upset."

Maddie heaved out a sigh, her eyes automatically traveling to Mildred's scarred house on the hill. "Do you want to take a walk with me?"

If George found her desire to change the subject strange, he didn't show it. "I guess. Where are we going?"

"On a ghost hunt." Maddie saw no reason to lie. "The story about what happened yesterday is pretty long and convoluted. At the center of it, though, is a ghost."

"Mildred? The woman who lived in the house, right? I heard she died. I'm sorry about that if you knew her."

Maddie shook her head. "It wasn't Mildred. It was someone else."

"Who?"

"I honestly have no idea."

George merely shrugged and nodded. "Sure. A ghost hunt sounds good. As long as I get to spend some time with you, I don't care what we do."

Maddie's smile was genuine as she snagged his gaze. "I guess we have a plan then, huh?"

"We certainly do."

"THIS IS THE PLACE."

Nick double-checked the address on his GPS with the numbers on the ramshackle house and shook his head. After leaving the morgue, Kreskin suggested heading to Gaylord to talk to the one family tie they'd been able to confirm for Mildred. It was a nephew, although Nick and Kreskin could find no proof the man ever spent time with his aunt.

"You're sure this is the place?" Nick remained dubious as he regarded the rundown home. It was set back from the road, garbage strewn about the driveway, and the house didn't exactly look hospitable. "Maybe there's a mistake in the record."

"There's only one way to find out." Kreskin was resigned as he got out of the patrol car, being careful to avoid the litter as he walked across what could loosely be described as a "lawn" and climbed the rickety steps that led to the front door of the house. "Let's see what we've got here."

Kreskin knocked and waited, Nick a few feet behind him. When the door finally opened, both men were surprised to see the clean-cut man standing on the other side of the threshold. He looked well-groomed and put together. He also looked confused.

"Can I help you?"

"Steven Wilkins?" Kreskin asked, glancing at his phone for confirmation on the name before continuing.

The man nodded. "That's me. Can I help you?"

"Oh, well, I hope so." Kreskin slid his phone inside his pocket and turned to business. "Do you have an elderly aunt who lives in Blackstone Bay?"

Now it was Steven's turn to be confused. "Technically. My father has a sister – her name is Mildred – and she lives in Blackstone Bay. I haven't seen her in years, though."

"I see." Kreskin exchanged a quick look with Nick, who opted to remain on the ground in case the stairs gave way, before continuing. "I regret to inform you that your aunt passed away last night."

Steven widened his eyes, surprise evident. "I ... well ... come in." He pushed open the door and took a step back.

Kreskin recognized he was taking a moment to regroup and did as he asked, Nick following a few seconds later. Even though the house was a mess outside, it was clean and neat inside. There was nothing out of place and the clutter from the lawn didn't stretch beyond the front door.

"I'm sorry about the mess outside," Steven offered absently as he led the men into a small kitchen and gestured toward the table. "I only moved here during the winter. I got a great deal on the house at auction because it was a foreclosure. I haven't had a chance to clean up the yard yet. It's been too cold."

"That's okay. I didn't even notice," Kreskin lied.

Steven snorted as he moved toward the counter. "Can I get you some coffee?"

"Sure," Kreskin replied. "That sounds nice." He settled at the table with Nick while Steven poured mugs of coffee for everybody. "I'm sorry about the loss of your aunt."

"Oh, well, if you want to know the truth, I've been trying to decide how I'm supposed to feel about that," Steven admitted. "In all honesty, I didn't know her very well. My father insisted we never speak to her and I can't remember the last time I saw her. I think it was at a family reunion when I was like ten or so."

"I don't want to pry, but why did your father not want you in contact with your aunt?" Kreskin asked, bobbing his head in thanks when Steven delivered the coffee.

"My father had a rather ... um ... prickly disposition," Steven replied. "He and my aunt had a falling out when their father died – and that was shortly after I was born, if I understand the timeline correctly – and they ended up saying some things they couldn't take back."

"Was it over money?" Nick asked.

Steven shrugged. "My family has never been what you would call well-to-do, which means zero to no inheritance for just about everyone, so I can't imagine it being over money. Of course, my father was cheap so it probably was about money. Knowing him, he probably burned his relationship with his sister over a couple thousand bucks. That sounds just like him."

Nick and Kreskin exchanged a weighted look.

"And your father is dead now, correct?" Kreskin queried.

Steven nodded. "He's been gone a few years now. I was in my late thirties and I'm forty-two now so I guess he's been gone almost five years. It seems shorter than that for some reason."

"And you didn't try to get in touch with your aunt after the fact?" Kreskin asked.

"No, and I'm sure you think that makes me a terrible person." Steven warmed his hands on his coffee mug. "I didn't know her, though. It wasn't as if my father was an ogre keeping me away from a nice woman. The few memories I have of Aunt Mildred are terrible. She wasn't nice to me. In fact, I remember her threatening to smack me around with a hose once."

The statement stirred a memory in Nick. "When I was a kid, my best friend lived about a block or so away from Mildred. We played in the woods behind both houses. She threatened me with the hose a time or two, as well. I think that was simply her way."

"Well, as a kid, all I knew is that my father thought she was evil and she was mean to me," Steven explained. "I didn't have any hate for the woman, but she was a virtual stranger to me."

"Still, you must have known a little something about her," Kreskin prodded. "We're having trouble tracking down family records. We have Stanley Dombrowski on record as her husband, but apparently she changed back to her maiden name after his death.

They were married a long time, but he died on the job a couple decades ago."

"Yeah, there's some sort of story that goes along with that death." Steven scratched his ear. "I'm trying to remember. I think he was in forestry or something and a tree fell on him."

Nick's eyebrows hopped. "Wow. I never heard that story."

"I think it was before your time," Kreskin supplied. "I don't think you were born yet ... or at least it was close. I honestly don't remember the story very well either. I was a teenager when it was fresh in the Blackstone Bay gossip circles. I remember some of the women – my mother included – were scandalized when Mildred went back to her maiden name. They didn't think it was right."

"My how times change," Nick drawled. "Now it's normal for women to keep their maiden names. I'm still not sure if Maddie is going to take my name when we get married."

"I'm sure you guys will work it out." Kreskin focused on Steven. "I understand you weren't close with your aunt but there's something else you should know about her death. A young girl was found in the basement. She was fifteen. We're trying to figure out how she got there and why Mildred had her."

Steven's expression shifted from curious to astonished. "I'm not sure I understand."

"We're not sure we understand either," Nick said. "We're trying to ascertain if Mildred had any children. It's possible, given her age, that the birth might have been missed if she was young enough and had a home birth. Right now we have absolutely nothing to go on."

Steven tapped on his chin and shook his head. "I'm sorry. I never heard of Aunt Mildred having a child. She was younger than my father – oh, a good twelve or thirteen years, I think – so I'm pretty sure I would've known if she had a kid. That's not something the family would've been able to keep secret."

"That's what we were wondering." Kreskin kicked back in his chair. "It's a mess. I don't suppose you could tell us everything you remember about your aunt, could you? I know that's probably not much, but we have to start somewhere."

Steven nodded without hesitation. "Anything to help. I hope you discover where that girl belongs. I'm just sick thinking that she's been left alone in this world. Let me think where to start, though. I'm not sure I can offer much, but I'm willing to help as much as possible."

"Take your time."

"THIS PLACE DOESN'T LOOK as bad as I feared," George said as they crested the hill that led to Mildred's house. "It looks like the roof burned through, but the rest of the structure doesn't look so bad."

"I talked to Nick on the way back from the children's home and he says whoever started the fire used an accelerant," Maddie explained, her eyes keen as she searched the bare foliage for a hint of ghostly movements. "The fire spread up but not down so, other than water damage, the house isn't in terrible condition."

"It's in a good location." George glanced around, his gaze busy. "I mean ... I wouldn't want to keep this house, but I wonder how much the land will go for."

Maddie was confused by the conversational shift. "What do you mean?"

"Oh, well, I've been doing some thinking." George's cheeks flooded with color, something Maddie realized she got from him. It was a mannerism that she didn't learn but somehow inherited from a man she didn't know until recently. Her mother always hated it when she got to blushing over something stupid, but now Maddie realized it was because it reminded Olivia of her ex-husband.

"What have you been thinking?" Maddie was honestly curious.

"I've been thinking of buying a house here," George admitted, his gaze earnest when it snagged with Maddie's clear blue orbs. "I wanted to run the idea by you because it would mean seeing each other more often – and I can't guarantee I would get this parcel of land or anything, but I'm definitely interested because it's set back from town and yet still close to you – but I'm considering it depending on your reaction."

Maddie felt exposed. "I'm not sure I understand," she said after a beat. "Why do you need my permission?"

"Because we're just starting a relationship here and you're getting married," George replied. "I'm assuming – eventually, at least – that means there will be grandchildren. I can already picture Nick and you as parents and I don't want to miss that.

"Still, our relationship is a work in progress," he continued. "If you're not comfortable with me being so close, I understand. I don't want to be the source of added strain in your life."

Maddie licked her lips as she debated the statement. "I want you around."

George exhaled heavily, relieved. "Good."

"I don't want you around because you feel guilty, though," she clarified. "What I mean by that is you don't have to move here if you don't want to. I like the idea a lot, but this is a small town. You're used to bigger cities. In fact ... ." She trailed off.

"I left your mother and moved to a bigger city," George finished, guilt washing over him. "You're worried Blackstone Bay might not be big enough for me."

"I don't want you to feel penned in."

"I won't."

"How can you be sure?"

George sighed. He adored his daughter – she was everything he hoped she would grow up to be – but she had a fearful side that showed on occasion and he hated knowing that he might be partially responsible for it. His actions, however misguided, shaped Maddie as a young child. His abandonment made Olivia bitter and Maddie the worrying type. It was too late to take it back, though. He could only move forward.

"I'm sure." George was firm. "This area is busier than it was when I first visited. Gaylord and Traverse City aren't far away if I need to shop. Also, well, I'll still be working for at least another five years. That means, even if I make this my home base, I'll have some traveling to do. All of that travel will be to big cities. That's the nature of my business."

"I didn't think about that." Maddie tilted her head to the side, considering. "Do you really want to be that close to me?"

"Yes." George answered without hesitation. "I want to be as close to you as possible. I want to spend time with you, get to know you. I want to be at your wedding. I want to know your children. Basically, I want to be a better grandfather than I was a father."

Maddie's expression turned sympathetic. "We've talked about that. You know I don't blame you for what happened. Er, well, I don't blame you for all of it."

"I left."

"You came back, though. My mother wouldn't allow you in to see me. Part of this is on her, which is why she hasn't been around as much. I've seen glimpses of her, but it's almost as if she's feeling guilty. I wish she would get over it so we could talk and put it behind us, but she's being sulky."

George barked out a laugh, the sound taking Maddie by surprise. "I don't know a lot of fathers who boast daughters who can see dead people, but I think I'm starting to get used to it. I didn't even think it was a little weird when you mentioned your dead mother just now."

Maddie's smile was rueful. "Sorry. I know it's hard for you."

"No, it's hard for you," George corrected. "I'm your father. I'll support you no matter what."

Maddie beamed. "Well, that goes double for me. If you want to move here permanently and get out of the hotel, I think it's a great idea. In fact, I think you should look at buying this land. It will drive Granny crazy to know you're so close."

"Yes, that's an added bonus." George's eyes gleamed. "Don't mention it to her. I want to be the one to tell her if it comes to fruition."

Maddie giggled. "She'll probably steel herself to live forever if she knows you're close enough to stop in every day. I like this idea more and more."

"Yes, well, I have to call the bank." George turned serious as he eyed the house. "It's a great piece of land, but we don't know who owns it now, right?"

"We definitely don't," Maddie agreed. "I'm guessing it was paid for but ... it's weird. Mildred was our neighbor from the time I was born until yesterday. I know absolutely nothing about her, though."

"I'm guessing that look on your face means you're going to find out."

"Definitely."

"You're a treasure, Maddie." George slung an arm around his daughter's slim shoulders. "Never change."

"You sound like Nick."

"I'm going to take that as a compliment ... at least I think."

"You definitely should."

9. NINE

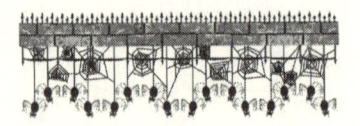

Nick texted about dinner. Since Maddie wasn't in the mood to cook, she suggested heading to the local diner. She decided to walk because it was a nice day and found Nick waiting for her in the parking lot when she arrived.

"You didn't have to wait out here," Maddie chided, amused despite herself. "You could've claimed our regular booth."

"I missed you too much to wait." Nick wrapped his arms around Maddie and held her tight, burying his face in her hair. "Hmm. You smell like pineapple."

Maddie patted his back, sensing right away that he'd had a long day. "It's a new body spray I picked up for the season. Do you like it?"

"I honestly wish they would make body spray so you could smell like pot roast." Nick's smile was crooked when he pulled back. "This is a nice second option, though."

Maddie snorted. "Believe it or not, I think they make body spray that smells like bacon."

"Sold."

"I'm not sure I want to go around smelling like a breakfast food, though."

Nick cocked his head, considering. "I'm not sure I want you going around smelling like bacon either now that I've had a chance to give it some thought. You already attract every man who lays eyes on you. If you smell like bacon, I'll have to carry a big stick around to beat them off."

Maddie chuckled as she linked her fingers with his, tugging him toward the door as she studied his face. "You look tired, Nicky."

"It's been a long day, love." Nick knew better than lying. "I have a lot to tell you."

"I have a few things to tell you, too."

"Let's get our regular booth and get to it." Nick squeezed her hand. "Hey, before that, though, I want to make sure you know I love you."

Maddie's antenna went up. "Is something bad about to happen?"

"No worse than usual. It simply struck me when I saw you walking up. You are – and always will be – the love of my life."

"Oh, right back at you."

NICK AND MADDIE OPTED for their favorite circular booth in the back corner of the diner. They preferred it because they could sit next to one another without looking like goofy morons. Maddie reached for the specials menu the second her bottom hit the vinyl seat.

"Oh, they have pot roast. Look at that."

Nick's smile was smug. "I know what I'm getting."

"I figured. I think I'm going with the spaghetti. They have the best sauce here."

"Knock yourself out."

The diner's owner, Ruby, approached the table with a harried expression on her face and an order pad in her hand. Maddie and Nick weren't bothered by her demeanor. They'd known her for the better part of their lives and understood she was more bark than bite.

"What will it be?"

"Spaghetti and iced tea," Maddie answered perfunctorily. "Also, could you add extra mushrooms to the sauce if it's not too much trouble?"

"Sure." Ruby flicked her eyes to Nick. "Pot roast? You were practically salivating over it when you stopped in to pick up your lunch."

Maddie shot Nick a derisive look. "I knew you were up to something when you said you wanted me to smell like pot roast."

Ruby let loose a guttural laugh. "Yeah, he's not good when it comes to manipulation, is he?"

"I want iced tea, too," Nick said, resting his arm against the back of the booth, his expression serious. "Let me ask you something, Ruby, did you ever know Mildred Wilkins to have kids?"

Ruby didn't bother hiding her surprise at the question. "No. Why? Should I know about kids?"

"I don't know. We're just checking on a few things and we can't seem to find a complete listing of her family members for some reason."

"Mildred always was the private sort." Ruby shifted from one foot to the other as she searched her memory. "You know, I honestly can't remember her coming in here more than a handful of times. She didn't seem sociable."

"I was trying to think back to any interactions I had with her over the years, too," Maddie admitted. "All I remember is her threatening Nick and me with a hose if we walked on her land while playing in the woods. For years I really thought she was going to whip me with a garden hose.

"Then I remember telling Granny about it one day and she was up in arms," she continued. "She marched down to the house and had a huge row with Mildred. I thought they might come to blows until Mom stepped in."

Nick smiled. "How did that end?"

Maddie shrugged. "I don't really remember. I know there was fighting and then Mom intervened. They stopped fighting after that, but I can't ever remember Granny and Mildred talking again. Granny did flip her the bird whenever we happened to pass by and Mildred was in the yard, though."

Ruby's laughter was so loud it caused a few heads to turn in their direction. "That sounds like Maude. She's always been a pip. As for

Mildred, I don't know what to tell you. I've never seen her with a kid."

"That seems to be the general consensus."

Ruby eyed Nick for a long beat. "Is this about the girl Maddie found in the basement?"

"How do you know about that?" Maddie asked, defensive. "Is that story making the rounds?"

"Of course it's making the rounds. You saved a little girl from a fire ... a girl that apparently had no reason to be in that basement. That's all anyone can talk about."

Maddie cast a sidelong look to Nick. "Is that why you're so tired?"

Nick forced a smile. "Partially. We were inundated with calls today. People from all over the state – some from out of state – and all are missing a daughter. Some are missing toddlers. Others are missing children who would be adults now. All want to know if we found their daughter in that house yesterday."

Maddie was flabbergasted. "Oh, Nicky. I ... what are you guys doing?"

"We're shuttling the calls to the state police," Nick answered without hesitation. "They can weed out the bulk of them. They're running evidence from inside Mildred's house as it is."

"But ... that girl, she called Mildred her grandmother," Maddie pointed out. "I don't think she was kidnapped ... at least not the way everyone else was assuming."

"I know." Nick was grave. "I read the report from Patty Foster. She sent over a description of what happened this afternoon at the children's home. I hear you were instrumental in getting Angel to talk, by the way. Good job."

Maddie didn't want to be complimented on a job well done. She wanted answers. "Do you have any idea who that girl is?"

"No, and we've got more questions than answers." He spared a glance for Ruby, a bit of warning extending outward, and then continued. "We found Mildred's nephew. He doesn't know a lot about his aunt because there was some sort of family feud. He was adamant she didn't have a child, though."

"What about someone else in the family?" Ruby was officially intrigued. "Don't worry about me spreading the gossip around, by the way. I wouldn't do that. The kid's well-being is the most important thing and everyone spreading her business around isn't going to help."

"We honestly don't know," Nick admitted. "As far as we can tell, Mildred had one brother. He died years ago. His son lives in Gaylord. He's a likable enough guy, but he wasn't a lot of help. I could tell he felt bad – and maybe even a little guilty because he never checked on his elderly aunt who lived alone – but he couldn't offer us more than a handful of stories."

"And none of those stories involved a kid, right?" Maddie pressed.

"No."

"So where did Angel come from?"

"I don't know." Nick squeezed her shoulder with the arm he draped over the back of the booth. "Right now, we started a search to see if we can find missing girls named 'Angel', or at least some variation on the name, and we'll go from there."

"Well, I'll put your orders in." Ruby looked disturbed as she shook her head. "This whole thing makes me sick to my stomach."

"You're not the only one." Nick waited until Ruby disappeared to lower his forehead to Maddie's, giving her a quick kiss before she could launch into a serious discussion. "Tell me about your day."

"What?"

"Tell me about your day," Nick repeated. "I'm sick of talking about my day. It was long and fruitless. You actually accomplished something. You got a terrified girl to open up and trust you."

"I also spent five hundred bucks on stuff for her at Target," Maddie admitted ruefully.

Nick chuckled. "I'm sure she'll appreciate it."

"She was really excited for the books and coloring stuff. She fought when it was time for me to leave again."

That was exactly what Nick was worried about. "Mad, you can't let that bother you. I know part of you is already so attached to her that it's going to be like pulling teeth when we find a permanent placement for her, but you cannot let this overwhelm you. I'm going to be really upset if you do."

"I won't let it overwhelm me," Maddie promised. "Angel made so much progress today it was amazing. I think she can speak, although she didn't try. She's not completely deaf. She can hear some of what we say. Right now she's only comfortable communicating through sign language, though."

"Hey, at least you figured it out. If you hadn't stopped to visit her, nothing might have come of that. We're a lot better off now than we were this morning."

"And to think, you didn't want me to visit her," Maddie teased. "I guess I was right and you were wrong, huh? I think I'm going to have to remind you of that later."

"Ha, ha." Nick gave Maddie's hair a playful tug.

"Well, well, well." A dismissive voice washed over the table, causing Maddie to internally sigh when she recognized it. "What do we have here? Why am I not surprised that you guys are still acting like goofy teenagers when it comes time to go out in public?"

Nick rolled his eyes as he turned to look at the area in front of the table. Marla Proctor, the woman who made it her mission to annoy Maddie at every turn, stood in a prominent position and glared at the couple. Her sidekick, Cassidy Dunham, stood about two feet back and looked less certain.

"Good evening, Marla," Nick drawled, disdain evident. "I'm surprised the nuthouse let you out for the night. Or, wait, did you escape? Should I call the nice men in white coats to collect you?"

Maddie pressed her lips together to keep from laughing.

"Oh, your wit astounds me," Marla deadpanned. "I can't believe you didn't go for the career in comedy before becoming a cop. Or, wait, maybe you became a cop because you're so bad at it that it becomes inadvertently funny."

Maddie immediately bristled. "You take that back!"

"Settle down, tiger." Nick kept a firm grip on her shoulder to make sure Maddie didn't launch herself across the table in an effort to scratch out Marla's eyes. "I appreciate that you're ready to stand up for me at the drop of a hat, but it's really not necessary. This is Marla. Everyone knows that she speaks complete and utter nonsense."

Maddie remained stiff. "She shouldn't say that about you. You're a good cop."

"Don't let her get to you, Mad," Nick admonished. "That's exactly what she wants. She clearly feels she's not getting enough attention today so she stopped by our table because even negative attention will do."

"Oh, stuff it." Marla made a face. "I stopped by your table because I'm looking for information on the girl who was found in Mildred's house. Do you have any leads on her yet?"

Maddie was instantly suspicious. "Why do you care?"

"I'm naturally curious," Marla replied. "I thought I might volunteer my help – perhaps run a fundraiser or something for the little darling – but I need to be able to track her down if I expect to do that."

Nick quickly joined Maddie in the suspicious department. "I'm not telling you anything about her. If that's why you came over here, you can just toddle off in the other direction." He made a dismissive gesture with his fingers. "In fact, if you could toddle off regardless, that would be great. Maddie and I are trying to have a romantic dinner and four is most definitely a crowd."

"Oh, you wish you could have a romantic dinner with me," Marla shot back.

Nick mimed vomiting, causing Maddie to squeeze his knee under the table.

"Don't let her drag you into an immature face off," Maddie warned, slowly letting her eyes shift to Marla. "As for you, you might as well mind your own business. You're not involved in this. Don't you have a job to do or something?"

"Of course I do. I'm a philanthropist at heart, though."

Maddie and Nick snorted in unison, prodding Cassidy to step forward. She looked nervous as she wrung her hands together. Since she was the one in a relationship with Nick when Maddie came back to town – a relationship Nick promptly ended, resulting in a broken heart and embarrassment for Cassidy – any interaction between the threesome was always strained.

"She really does want to help," Cassidy prodded. "She's not making it up."

Nick ran his tongue over his teeth as he debated how to answer. "Cassidy, I really don't want to turn this into a fight. Things have been quiet for months between us and I like it that way. I'm not giving Marla private information about that girl, though. It's simply not going to happen."

Cassidy had the grace to look abashed. "I don't know that we're looking for private information," she hedged. "It's more that we're looking for direction. We want to help, but we need to know where to aim ourselves to do it."

"Oh, you don't want to help," Maddie countered. "Marla has figured out a way to get attention for herself from whatever it is you've got planned and you're just tagging along for the ride because you're her sidekick and Marla can't function if she doesn't have someone to boss around."

Nick lifted an eyebrow, amused. "That was catty, Mad."

"Really?" Maddie was taken aback. "Too catty?"

Nick made a feline growling noise and smiled. "Just catty enough. I liked it."

"Oh, you make me sick." Marla was beside herself. "You can't keep that girl's identity and whereabouts to yourself. It's against the law if other people want to help. I happen to know that Maddie was over there visiting her this afternoon – Christy went with her and told people at the salon – so you obviously told her where to find the girl. Now you have to tell me."

Nick rubbed his jaw with his free hand, confused where to start. "Well, um, you're stupid."

Maddie ducked her head to avoid Marla's mutinous stare.

"Maddie is part of my investigative team," Nick explained, relishing the hateful look on Marla's face as she tossed back her hair. "She found the girl and bonded with her. She's necessary to the information process. As far as I can tell, you're not necessary for anything.

"As for sharing information, you've got that wrong," he continued. "It's against the law for me to share information with those not directly involved with the case. That includes you."

Cassidy was the first to speak. "Since when is Maddie a part of your investigation team? You never allowed me to tag along when you were on a case."

Nick stared at her a beat, conflicted. "Maddie is part of the team because she was there last night."

"Maddie has been helping you with cases since she got back, though," Marla argued. "It seems to me there's one set of rules for Maddie and another set of rules for everybody else. It's not fair."

Nick merely shrugged. "If that's the way you feel, I guess you're entitled to your beliefs. It doesn't really matter to me, though."

"That's it?" Marla was incredulous. "You're just going to ignore my question."

"Pretty much."

"Fine." Marla straightened her shoulders. "I'll go to Dale. He'll tell me."

Nick tried – and failed – to bury a snort. "Good luck with that. I'm sure he'll be as happy to see you as I am. In fact ... ." Whatever he was about to say died on his lips as Christy, her red hair wild, stormed into the restaurant and stopped in front of Maddie. "Is something wrong?"

Christy ignored Nick and kept her focus on Maddie. "Well, I hope you're happy!" She shoved what looked like a white pen across the table. "You were right and my life is now over."

Nick was understandably confused. "What is that?" He leaned over Maddie's shoulder and frowned. "Is that a pen?"

Maddie swallowed hard. "It's a pregnancy test."

"And it's positive," Christy screeched. "You were right and now the world is coming to an end. I blame you!"

"Uh-oh." Nick was beyond amused as Maddie's expression twisted. "I'm going to be an uncle, huh? This day is starting to look up."

10. TEN

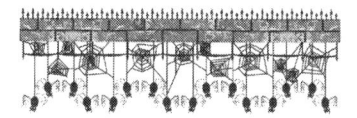

"I swear I was kidding when I teased her about it."

Maddie and Nick were still talking about Christy's surprising news the next morning as they made their way to the main floor to start breakfast preparations.

"Oh, come on," Nick protested, digging in the refrigerator for eggs, bacon and hash browns. "You had to legitimately suspect you were right."

Maddie tilted her head to the side as she poured water into the coffee machine. "I ... don't think so. I was just kidding. Honest."

"You have a very honest face." Nick gave her a quick kiss before grabbing a skillet from the cupboard. "Still, I think you might have used your abilities to ferret out information without evening realizing it."

Maddie was stunned silent by the suggestion. Maude, however, was the opposite.

"What abilities is Maddie using and what gossip did she ferret out?" Maude asked as she glided into the room. She looked well-rested, which made Nick believe she'd spent the evening relaxing rather than vandalizing. "Tell me now."

Nick regarded her for a long beat before shaking his head. "I'm not sure we should tell you. The news will be all over town if we do."

Maddie found her voice. "The news will be all over town no matter what. Cassidy and Marla heard what she said. I'm actually surprised the news hasn't already filtered back to Granny."

"Good point." Nick's expression was serious as he regarded Maude. "Christy is pregnant."

Maddie widened her eyes to comical proportions. "Wow. You turned quickly on that one, huh? Not two seconds ago you said we should keep it secret and now you just blurted it out like it was nothing."

Nick shrugged, unbothered. "Like you said, everybody already knows."

"I don't think John knows."

Nick's smile turned evil. "How bad would it be if I were the one to tell him?"

"Very bad." Maddie lightly smacked Nick's arm but her tone meant business. "It's up to Christy to tell John. That's their ... thing."

"Christy is pregnant?" Maude accepted the mug of coffee Maddie slid her way and settled at the end of the kitchen table to absorb the news. "That's ... wow. Did she seem excited?"

"Furious would be the more appropriate word," Nick replied as he used a spatula to flip hash browns. "Apparently Maddie was teasing her earlier in the day about being pregnant and Christy thought it was ridiculous. Then she took a pregnancy test and realized it wasn't so ridiculous."

"Oh, well ... I guess that's nice." Maude didn't look convinced. "It's a little soon for them to be having kids."

"I think they'll be fine." Nick wasn't particularly bothered by the notion of being an uncle. "John will probably freak out for a bit – that is his way – but I'll talk him down. Don't worry."

Maddie shot Nick a knowing look. "You're dying to mess with him about this, aren't you?"

"The guy who swore up and down that he was never going to settle down? Yeah, I'm dying to mess with him."

Maddie stilled. "Wait ... are you saying John never wants to settle down?"

Nick realized what he said too late to take it back. "I'm saying that up until he started seriously dating Christy a few months ago that John was more reticent about a long-term relationship that involved kids," he hedged. "That doesn't seem to be the case now, but I don't believe that he'll take the news particularly well."

Maddie couldn't stop the worry from bubbling up. "You don't think he would abandon her to raise the baby on her own, do you?"

"Of course not." The words were out of Nick's mouth before he gave them much thought. After a moment of contemplation, though, he became more convinced that he was right. "That won't happen. He's going to freak out but do the right thing."

Maddie wasn't even remotely placated. "Because he wants to be with Christy or because he knows your mother and father will beat the crap out of him if he doesn't comply?"

"I ... what's the difference?"

"There's a big difference." Maddie's tone turned cold. "I wouldn't want you to marry me, to settle down, if the only reason you did it was because of a baby. I would want you to love me."

Nick felt as if he'd inadvertently walked into a trap. "Mad, I do love you."

"I'm talking about John and Christy."

"I think John loves Christy," Nick offered. "It's soon, but I see it when he looks at her. You don't have to worry about this. It's going to work out. Trust me."

Maddie wanted to believe him, but her agitation level was high. "He'd better love her. I'm going to smack him around if he doesn't."

"I'll help you." Nick looked to Maude for help. He was anxious for a shift in conversation. "What about you? What gossip do you have?"

"Actually, I do have some gossip you might be interested in," Maude acknowledged. "As for Christy, don't worry about it, Maddie girl. Christy is going to be a fabulous mother and once he says and does two or three stupid things, John is going to be a terrific father. He and Christy love each other even though it's new. You don't have anything to worry about."

Maddie didn't say anything, causing Maude and Nick to exchange a quick look before the conversation turned in a different direction.

"As for my gossip, I think you'll definitely be interested," she said. "I was talking to a few people last night and apparently there was a rumor that Mildred was pregnant at one time."

Nick perked up. "Seriously?"

Maude nodded. "Now, this was about forty years ago," she cautioned. "It might even be a little bit longer than that. Pinning down the exact timeframe isn't easy."

"I understand that. What have you got?"

"Well, Mildred got a little fat there for a bit and did her best to keep away from everyone else," Maude volunteered. "That wasn't out of the ordinary because she didn't like to hang with anybody other than her best friend at the time, but a few people caught a glimpse of her and thought she looked pregnant."

"Was this before or after her husband died?" Nick asked.

"Before."

"What about a baby?" Maddie challenged. "If she looked pregnant, she must've had a baby on her hip not long after."

Maude shook her head, her lips curving down. "No. We never saw her with a baby."

Maddie turned to Nick for answers. "What do you think that means?"

Nick opted for honesty. "I don't know what it means. You don't either so don't let your imagination get away from you. Right now all we have is a bunch of gossipy women who thought she looked fat. She might've simply gained a few extra pounds or something."

Maddie was dubious. "Looking pregnant and appearing fat are two entirely different things."

"Fair enough." Nick narrowed his eyes on Maude's face. "Did anyone ever ask her about it?"

"No. She didn't like people. She wasn't social. That's not something you just blurt out."

"Right." Nick was thoughtful as he flipped hash browns. "Even if she didn't give birth, there are several options. She could've lost the baby at some point, in which case it's a tragedy. It could've been a stillbirth. Or she could've given the baby up for adoption because she didn't believe she was capable of taking care of it."

"How does that play into what's happening now?" Maddie was legitimately curious. "I mean ... do you think she gave the baby up and somehow Angel has ties to that baby?"

"I honestly don't know, Mad."

"Is there a way we can find out?"

"Common practices forty years ago would suggest to me that Mildred had the baby in a hospital," Nick noted. That was the seventies. People were mostly having babies in hospitals then and records of live births were kept. We should be able to track it down."

"That seems like a lot of work."

"It does," Nick agreed, his expression thoughtful. "Maude, just out of curiosity, who was Mildred's best friend? The woman you said she spent time with but no one else."

"Oh, *that*." Maude's distaste was evident, her lip curling. "I should've realized you would fixate on that."

"Yes, you should have," Nick agreed. "Who was it?"

"You're not going to like it."

"I figured."

"It was Harriet Proctor," Maude volunteered. "She and Mildred were tight for a hot minute, although they eventually had a falling out. If anyone knows the secret Mildred was keeping at the time, it's probably Harriet."

"Oh, geez." Nick rubbed his forehead as he regarded Maddie. "That is so not how I want to spend my day."

Maddie took pity on him. "I'm going to try to find the ghost I saw at Mildred's house. I tried looking yesterday but got distracted when Dad said he was going to ask around about buying the property for building a house. I'm going back today."

"That sounds good." Nick was distracted. "Be careful up there and don't go into the house. It's not safe."

"I have no interest in going into the house."

"Keep it that way."

Maude wrinkled her forehead as she considered what Maddie

said. "Wait ... is George seriously considering moving down the street from us? We can't allow that. No way. No how."

Nick shot her a stern look. "You stay out of that part."

"No."

Maddie finally realized what Nick and Maude were talking about. "No, Nicky is right. You stay out of it, Granny. Dad wants to move to town and I like the idea. Don't do anything annoying to make him change his mind."

Maude wasn't about to be bullied. "I'll do what I think is right."

Nick extended a warning finger. "I don't care how much I love you. I will arrest you if it comes to it."

Maude rolled her eyes. "I have no intention of getting caught."

"Oh, well, that makes me feel better."

"Good."

"I was being sarcastic."

"You'll live."

MADDIE LEFT A FUMING Maude to plot her attack on George not long after Nick left for work. She knew she would have to sit down and have a discussion with her grandmother before all was said and done but now wasn't the time. George didn't even know if buying the property was something he could swing so there was no sense getting worked up until they had more information. The fight over George's proximity would have to wait for later.

Maddie was much more interested in thinking about Christy's pregnancy. She was excited at the prospect of having a baby to dote over – especially one that would be a niece or nephew – but she couldn't help being worried about John's reaction. He wasn't Nick ... by a long shot. Maddie had no doubt if she turned up tomorrow and told Nick she was pregnant that he would react with love and joy. John was another story, though. He suffered from wanderlust. Maddie was genuinely worried he would take off out of fear. He wasn't a bad man, but he often did ridiculously stupid stuff.

"Why are you back here?"

Maddie jolted at the voice, turning swiftly and finding the ghost who pointed her toward Angel floating close to a tree at the west side of Mildred's property. She sucked in a breath, forced her heart rate to drop a bit, and mustered a smile. "Looking for you."

The woman didn't appear happy with the answer. "Why? You should be taking care of Angel."

Well, that answered that question, Maddie mused. "How do you know Angel?"

"What does it matter?" The ghost was an unhappy woman. There was no getting around that. The look she shot Maddie was straight out of a horror movie. "Why do you even care who I am? How can you see me at all?"

Maddie held her palms out and shrugged. "I've been able to see ghosts since I was a kid. It's an ability I was born with. You're not the first and I'm certain you won't be the last."

"Oh, well, how lucky for me."

Maddie ignored the sarcasm. "I saw Angel yesterday, by the way. She's doing much better."

Even though the woman did her best to appear blasé, Maddie sensed a change in her demeanor. "What do you mean? Why wouldn't she be doing okay?"

"Well, she was in rough shape when I discovered her," Maddie reminded the ghost. "She wasn't talking."

"Well ... ."

"We know she uses sign language to communicate," Maddie interjected quickly. "We know that she's at least partially deaf."

"She can hear some things," the woman said quickly. "The doctors say that might get even better if she gets the proper hearing aid."

Maddie filed that information away to dwell on later. "That's good to know. I'll tell the social worker. What I want to know now is how this all happened."

The ghost balked. "How did what happen? I didn't start the fire, if that's what you're asking."

"I know you didn't." Maddie feigned patience even though her irritation was growing with each word. "The fire was purposely set, though. Do you know how that happened?"

The ghost didn't answer the question, something Maddie found suspicious. Instead, she changed the subject. "Tell me about Angel. Where is she? Where are they keeping her? Is she okay? Is she traumatized?"

Something about the woman's manic desire to hear about Angel touched Maddie's heart. "She's okay. Once we realized she was trying to communicate with sign language, we got a professional to visit with her. We started talking to her a bit, got her to take a shower and wash her hair, and now it's something of a work in progress.

"I picked her up some clothes at the store yesterday," she continued. "I got her coloring books, something to read, and a few crossword puzzle games. Some of the things she says don't make sense. Like ... she called Mildred her grandmother."

"So?" The ghost bristled. "What's wrong with that?"

"There's nothing wrong with it," Maddie said hurriedly. "I love my grandmother dearly even though she's a massive pain in the butt sometimes. Grandmothers are great. The thing we're confused about is that we can't find a record of Mildred ever giving birth to a child."

Maddie studied the ghost's reaction closely.

"I don't see how that matters," the ghost said finally. "Blood doesn't determine a family. Why does it matter exactly how they were related?"

"It doesn't," Maddie replied. "There are rumors that Mildred was pregnant at one time, though. This would've been forty years ago." Maddie did the math in her head as she regarded the woman. "If Mildred did give birth, she didn't raise the baby. There's conjecture that maybe she gave the baby up for adoption."

"So?"

"We're simply trying to unravel all the answers," Maddie said quietly. "For example, is there perhaps a chance that you're the baby who was given up for adoption?"

The ghost stared at Maddie for a long beat, her expression remaining completely frozen. Finally, when she did speak, it was with frustration. "You're focusing on the wrong thing. It doesn't matter who was related to whom or how. What's important is keeping Angel safe. What's important is getting her away from all of this."

Maddie was understandably confused. "Getting her away from all of what?"

"All of ... this!" The ghost was clearly frustrated. "You need to focus on Angel and let go of the rest. It doesn't matter. In fact ... ." She turned and stared at the trees kitty-corner from where they stood. Her gaze was heavy and dark. "You need to leave now."

Maddie was confused. "Why?"

"You really need to go." The ghost made shooing motions with her hands. "Right now. It's not safe for you here."

Maddie flicked her eyes to the spot the ghost stared, her shoulders jerking when she heard the unmistakable sound of a twig cracking. Her heart skipped a beat and her anxiety spiked. "Is someone over there?"

"You need to leave right now." The ghost was firm. "I mean ... right now. Run. Go back to your house or the nearest point of safety. Whatever you do, don't stay here."

Maddie had a choice. She could move forward and search the woods to see if someone really was spying on her. She felt mildly idiotic fearing something she couldn't see. She could feel something, though, and whatever it was caused a shiver to run down her spine.

That's why she opted for the second choice. She immediately turned on her heel and broke into a run. She was in great shape – better than almost anyone she knew – and she focused on that as she put distance between Mildred's house and herself.

If someone was there, if someone was a threat, Maddie wouldn't allow herself to become a victim. She was smarter than that.

So, she put her head down and ran. She didn't turn back until she was at her house. By then, she was too far away to see anything. She could still feel the anger she originally brushed up against at Mildred's house, though.

Someone was extremely unhappy. If Maddie had to guess, that someone was exactly who they were looking for.

11. ELEVEN

Maddie immediately called Nick to tell him what happened while she was at the house. He told her to stay put and lock the doors before heading to check out the situation. By the time he slid his key in the door, Maddie was on pins and needles and practically threw herself on him when he crossed the threshold of her store.

"Did you find anything?"

Nick pulled her in for a tight hug and pressed a kiss to her cheek. "No, Mad. I didn't find anyone loitering out there and I'm not exactly a tracker so I don't know how to find footprints in the woods."

"Oh."

Nick smoothed her hair. "You're sure you didn't see anyone, right?"

Maddie nodded. "I'm sure. It was just a feeling. Plus, well, the ghost basically told me to run. I didn't give it much thought. Maybe I should've stayed behind to see who it was."

Nick vehemently shook his head. "Absolutely not, Mad. You did the right thing. Your safety is my number one priority."

Maddie tilted her head back and stared into his eyes. "I know. I was just ... talking. Now that I'm here ... and safe ... I feel a bit ridiculous. What if I imagined everything that happened?"

"I would rather you call me to check on a possibility of an overactive imagination than have something happen to you. I never want anything to happen to you. Not ever."

Maddie couldn't stop herself from smiling. "Me either."

Nick graced her with a soft kiss. "So, what's up next for you, love?"

"I'm going to see Angel."

Nick scowled. "Why can't you just open your shop and stay here? You haven't been open all week."

"It's been two days." Maddie refused to be drawn into a fight. "I've had other things on my mind. If you want me to give you an accounting of my time and a copy of my bank account balances to show I'm not running at a deficit, I can have that waiting when you get home tonight."

Nick narrowed his eyes. "Don't pick a fight."

"I was just about to warn you about doing the same thing."

Nick heaved out a sigh as he dragged a restless hand through his hair. "Fine. I won't pick a fight. You need to be careful and watch your back when you're running around, though. Also, you can't go back to Mildred's house looking for a ghost without back-up. I'm putting my foot down."

Maddie pressed her lips together to keep from laughing. "You're putting your foot down, huh?"

Nick glared. "You know what I mean."

"I do. You don't have to worry about that." Maddie honestly meant it. "I'm still going to visit Angel. I want to see her."

"Then visit Angel." Nick briefly rested his forehead against Maddie's. "You be safe while you're out and about, though. Watch your back ... and front ... and every other part of you because I happen to be attached to the entire package."

"I promise I'll be safe."

"You do that."

KRESKIN WAS FLIPPING THROUGH files when Nick returned to the police station. He barely glanced up when his partner let loose a weary groan as he sank into his chair.

"How are things on the domestic front?"

Nick arched an eyebrow as he regarded his partner. "Do you ever think women were put here simply to drive us nuts?"

Kreskin barked out a laugh. "I don't know. I never really considered it before. Obviously you believe that."

"I really do." Nick stretched out his legs. "Maddie thought someone was watching her while she was over at Mildred's house. She didn't see anyone, but she felt as if someone was spying."

Kreskin lifted his eyes, intrigued. "Did you find anything?"

"No, but I tend to believe Maddie's instincts."

"Yes, well, Maddie has good instincts." Kreskin saw no reason to lie. "Do you think someone was really watching her?"

Nick opened his mouth but didn't immediately answer.

"What are you thinking?" Kreskin prodded.

"I'm not sure." Nick saw no reason to cover up his feelings when it came to his partner. "If Maddie thinks someone was watching her, I have to believe she's right. She's rarely wrong on stuff like this and I don't want her questioning herself. She did the right thing by running. She's home and safe. I want her to have faith in herself so ... yeah, I think someone was really watching her."

"Who?"

Nick shrugged. "That is the question, isn't it? I think we should go over everything we have from start to end. We need a direction to point ourselves."

"That sounds good to me." Kreskin was all business as he squared his shoulders. "Let's put together a timeline and go from there."

ANGEL SEEMED TO KNOW Maddie was coming to visit because she was bouncing around her room when Maddie opened the door.

"Hello." Maddie saluted, which is essentially what Patty taught her to do in greeting. "How are you today?"

Angel's hands moved so fast Maddie could do nothing but widen her eyes.

"She says she's been enjoying the books you brought her," Patty supplied from her spot at the small desk in the corner of the room, her smile wide. "She's a big fan of the crossword puzzle books, too."

"Oh, well, I'm glad you like them." Maddie made sure she was facing Angel and that she talked slowly. She was convinced the girl could read lips. "How was your night?"

Angel shrugged.

"It was good," Patty translated. "I slept straight through. Do you know when I can leave? I don't want to stay here." Patty frowned when she was finished speaking and began signing for Angel's benefit. "We talked about this. You're stuck here for at least a little while. We don't know if you have any family out there or where you're going to end up just yet.

"I know you don't like it when I say things like that, but we agreed to be honest with each other," she continued. "You're kind of in limbo right now. I get that it's not easy or what you want, but we have to work with what we've got."

"Actually, that's one of the reasons I'm here," Maddie volunteered, smiling as she patted Angel's bed to prod the girl to sit next to her. "I know you said that Mildred was your grandmother and that's exclusively how you knew her, but there has to be more to the story."

Patty didn't bother translating. "I've tried to get more information out of her regarding that, too, but it hasn't been easy. I don't know if it's that she doesn't trust us enough yet to tell us or that she honestly doesn't know."

Maddie kept her eyes on Angel's serene face. Now that she was clean and in age-appropriate clothing she looked older than Maddie initially guessed upon finding her. She was still ridiculously small and Maddie felt the urgent need to fatten her up, but that would come with time.

"Angel, it's important we understand how you ended up with Mildred." Maddie's voice was gentle, her expression kind. "It wasn't always like that, right? There was a time you lived somewhere else. I'm sure of that."

Angel wrinkled her nose and looked at Patty as she began moving her hands. This time the conversation was much slower and Maddie could tell the girl was reluctant to share her private business.

"I don't know how long I was there," Patty started. "It felt like a long time. It was hard for me to keep track of the days because they all melted together."

Maddie nodded encouragingly. "I get that. The thing is, you had to come from somewhere. Tell me about your mother."

Angel adamantly shook her head.

"You have to," Maddie pressed. "We're working really hard to figure out where you came from. It hasn't been easy because Mildred was a private person. I lived fairly close to her for the bulk of my life and I don't think I talked to her more than ten times.

"If you want to know the truth, when I was growing up, everyone in the neighborhood said she was a mean lady and they didn't like her," she continued. "You were living with her. Is that how you felt?"

Angel worked her jaw, frustration evident. When she finally began signing it was with a hint of anger.

"She wasn't mean," Patty offered.

"What was she?" Maddie asked.

"Afraid," Patty answered as she watched Angel's hands.

Maddie and Patty exchanged a quick look before Maddie pushed forward. "What was she afraid of?"

"What would happen if people found out I was with her."

"But ... how did you end up with her?" Maddie couldn't let it go. "We never saw you outside. I essentially live next door to Mildred even though there's a lot of distance between the houses. I run a lot, though, and I'm in the woods on a regular basis as long as the weather allows for it. If you were ever outside, I can't help but think I would've seen you."

Angel swallowed hard, uncertainty etched on her young face.

"It's okay." Maddie rested her hand on Angel's shoulder. "I know this is hard for you. No, I really do. You're in a terrible position here, but you've got to trust someone. This isn't a world you can traverse alone and Patty and I really want to help you."

"That's true," Patty agreed. "We want to make sure you have the best life you can possibly have."

"The thing is, Angel, I spent some time at the library before coming here and I came up empty. I was trying to research Mildred's family tree," Maddie offered, changing tactics. "The branches are few and far between. Mildred had a brother that she wasn't close with. I can't find any children. Despite that, there's a rumor that Mildred was pregnant about forty years ago.

"That would've put her right around forty herself when she was pregnant if it's true," she continued. "No one ever saw her with a baby. So, the theory is that either something tragic happened or she gave the baby up for adoption."

"Oh." Realization dawned on Patty. "You're wondering if she gave up the baby and if Angel is somehow related to that baby."

Maddie nodded. "It makes sense, at least in a weird sort of way. Maybe Angel is her granddaughter, and Mildred was trying to help out the child she gave up all those years ago. I honestly don't know if that's the case but trying to dig up family records has been unbelievably hard."

"It's also possible that Angel isn't related to Mildred by blood at all," Patty pointed out. "We took a sample yesterday after you left, but it could take weeks to run a DNA test."

"I know." Maddie was resigned. "We need help figuring things out and I'm afraid you're the only one who can help us, Angel. You need to trust someone. I really wish it would be us."

Angel pursed her lips as she regarded the two women. When she finally began signing, it was with precision.

"I'll think about it," Patty translated, amused despite herself. "I guess that's our cue to let it go for a little bit."

Maddie tried not to be too bitter. "Yeah. I guess so."

NICK WASN'T SURPRISED when his brother strode through the door to his office. He'd been expecting a visit since Christy dropped her bomb the previous night. What did surprise him was that John took so long to react.

"Hello, Daddy," Nick called out, amusement positively dripping from his tongue.

John's expression was one for the record books. It promised retribution with a hint of mayhem. "That is not funny."

"You should try looking at things from where I'm sitting," Nick countered.

"Do I even want to know what you two are fighting about this time?" Kreskin asked wearily.

"No," John automatically answered.

"Yes." The gleam in Nick's eyes was evil. "It seems John and Christy are going to be parents. I believe my brother received the happy news yesterday."

"Really?" Kreskin lowered the report he was reading, Mildred's history all but forgotten. "You're going to be a father? Congratulations. I thought for sure Nick and Maddie would be the first to jump on the procreation train."

"We're fine waiting for a little bit," Nick supplied. "We want to get married before we add kids to the mix. It will happen – and probably sooner rather than later – but it doesn't need to happen right now. John always had to be first to do practically everything when we were kids so I'm not at all surprised about this."

"Ha, ha." John's expression was more misery than anything else. "How long have you known?"

Nick sobered. He recognized the slant of his brother's shoulders and knew that there was more going on here than fear. "I found out when Maddie did. Christy barreled into the diner last night and showed us the test. She seemed ... worked up."

"Oh, do you think?" John rubbed the back of his neck as he claimed the seat across from Nick's desk. "She threw that thing at me the minute I walked through the door last night."

Nick was philosophical. "Well, it wasn't very big so it couldn't have hurt much."

"No, but you know how those things work, right? She had to pee on it to run the test. She threw that at my head."

Nick fought the mad urge to laugh. "I hadn't exactly put that together. I'm sorry if it hurt your feelings."

"It didn't hurt my feelings," John shot back, his anger ratcheting up a notch. "It totally ripped my feelings apart and made me want to run as far away from this town as I can get."

"Oh, that's not an option." In truth, Nick was expecting this. John's fight-or-flight response was always on display. He usually chose flight first and fight second. He had no intention of allowing that to happen this time. "I sold you my house upon the condition that you stay in town. You can't sell or rent it to anyone else. You have no choice but to stay."

The look John shot his brother was full of malice. "Are you trying to kill me?"

"Not last time I checked."

"You think this is funny, don't you?" John's temper was on full display. "You think it's funny that I'm going to be a father."

"I think it's great that you're going to be a father," Nick clarified. "While Maddie and I plan to wait for a bit, I know I'll be beyond excited when it comes time to add to our family. I would think you'd feel the same way."

John's expression was withering. "You've been dating Maddie for almost a year, living with her for more than six months, planning to marry her since Christmas, and in love with her since kindergarten. Your situation is vastly different from my situation."

Nick honestly couldn't argue with the statement. "True, but love comes in different shapes and forms. I've seen you with Christy. I think you love her."

John balked. "We've only been dating a few months."

"More like six months," Nick corrected.

"No." John was adamant as he fervently shook his head. "We started out by flirting and not dating. Then we did some fighting that also wasn't associated with dating. We didn't start dating until the first of the year."

"Oh, that's crap." There was no way Nick intended to let his brother wiggle out of this situation via a semantics argument. "You guys might not have termed it dating until after Christmas because you were both acting goofy about the whole Christmas gift thing, but you were together before that. You were also exclusive before that.

"Quite frankly, Christy is the only woman you've been exclusive with for a very long time," he continued. "It's been years since you've even had a steady girlfriend."

"Christy is a good girl," Kreskin added. "She's fiery. You're lucky to have her."

"I agree," Nick said. "You're very lucky to have her."

John made a face. "I didn't say I wasn't lucky to have her."

"You're acting like it," Nick pointed out.

"No, I'm not. It's just ... ." John broke off, holding his hands palms up as a wave of helplessness washed over him. "I wasn't expecting this. I don't know what to do. I thought we would have time with each other just to screw around. You can't screw around if you're going to be parents. I'm pretty sure that's not allowed."

"No, you can't," Nick agreed. He found himself impressed with the fact that John seemed to have accepted the fact that he was going to be a father with minimal complaint. He wasn't trying to run from his responsibility – or Christy, for that matter – and that was a big step for a reformed playboy. Still, Nick could practically feel the desperation wafting from his brother. "It's not the end of the world. It's simply a new adventure."

"But ... I don't know how to do this." John's voice cracked. "Christy is just as worked up as me. She blames Maddie, for the record. She said she didn't even consider it until Maddie suggested it yesterday and that's why she took the test."

Nick was pragmatic. "Maddie might have prodded her to take the test, but she didn't get Christy pregnant. That's on you."

"Well, Christy is angry. She thinks Maddie did some sort of hoodoo on her or something."

"That sounds unlikely."

"Well, Christy isn't always rational under the best of circumstances," John supplied. "She tends to say whatever comes to her mind and then deals with the consequences after the fact. She's as freaked out as I am."

"That's actually good," Kreskin offered. "If you guys freak out now, have a rough few days and whatnot, then you can get over it together and move forward. You're going to have a lot to do before the baby arrives."

"For starters, you need to get Christy to a regular doctor," Nick pointed out. "She needs vitamins, a due date, and a check-up to make sure things are rolling right along."

"I know." John rolled his eyes. "She set up an appointment this afternoon."

"Oh. Is that why you decided to visit?"

"No. I'm here to see you. I thought you might have some sage advice for how to handle this situation."

"Why would I have sage advice?"

"Because you deal with the unexpected all the time," John replied. "Your girlfriend sees ghosts and saves random girls from fires. You should be used to this sort of thing."

"I'm pretty sure they're entirely different scenarios," Nick said dryly. "Still, you need to watch your mouth when you talk about Maddie. There's a reason she kept her secret for so long."

John had the grace to be abashed. "I didn't mean anything by it. I'm careful. Everyone here knows."

"Everyone here *does* know," Kreskin agreed. "You still need to be careful. As for a baby, I think you'll be a good father. You simply need to get your head out of your behind and get it together."

"And how do you suggest I do that?"

"I would start with heading out so you can go to Christy's appointment with her," Kreskin suggested without hesitation. "That's your baby, too. You should be there from the start."

John was taken aback. "Oh, well, I didn't even consider it."

"You really should." Nick's tone was gentle. "I know this has thrown you for a loop, but it really is going to be okay. Go with

Christy, show her you support her, and everything else will fall into place."

"I ... do you really think so?" John looked so hopeful it shook Nick to his very soul.

"I definitely think so." Nick bobbed his head. "It's going to be okay. I'll be here if you need help. Maddie will be here as soon as Christy calms down. It really will be okay."

"I hope so." John scrubbed the back of his neck. "This is a big deal."

"It is," Nick agreed. "You need to focus on Christy today, though. She needs you."

"I will."

"Good." Nick meant it. "After that, you'd better call Mom. If she hears she's going to be a grandmother through the Blackstone Bay gossip train she is not going to be happy."

John turned white and swallowed hard. "I didn't even think about that."

"Live in fear."

"Yeah. I think that's going to be my motto for the next nine months."

Nick's smile was chipper. "Oh, don't worry about that. Things will get better. I promise."

John could only hope his brother was right.

12. TWELVE

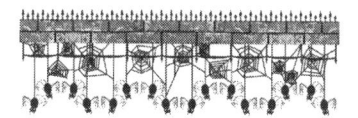

Angel's idea of "thinking about it" meant she actually intended to put a great deal of thought into her decision. That essentially meant she had no intention of reacting immediately.

Since Maddie wanted to give her the appropriate space, she stayed at the children's home for another hour before taking off and leaving Angel to her deep thoughts. Once back in Blackstone Bay, Maddie was at a loss. She couldn't return to Mildred's house for a ghost hunt unless she had backup. She knew George was out of town for the evening and Maude wasn't very good backup. That left Christy, and she had her own problems.

Instead of searching for the ghost, Maddie opted to do the one thing no one else wanted to do. It wasn't especially dangerous – at least physically – but Maddie knew she would never list it as a high point of her day. Still, it had to be done. Since Maddie had an opening in her schedule, she decided she would be the one take on the odious task.

She did her best not to appear amused as she parked in front of Harriet Proctor's house. Most of the toilet paper from two nights before had been removed, but a few errant strands located on the highest branches remained. For some reason, seeing toilet paper in the old oak tree tickled Maddie's funny bone and it took everything she had to refrain from laughing as she knocked on Harriet's front door.

To her utter astonishment (and disappointment), Marla was the one who opened the door. The two women narrowed their eyes at the same time, taking a moment to size one another up, and when Marla squared her shoulders and pushed out her chest Maddie knew that it was going to be an absolutely excruciating visit.

"What are you doing here?"

Maddie worked overtime to appear pleasant. "I was hoping to see your grandmother."

"And why would she want to see you?"

That was a fair question, Maddie internally conceded. Odds were that Harriet wouldn't want to see her. That didn't mean the visit wasn't important. Maddie decided on the spot that lying wasn't an option. Marla was annoying but intelligent. She would see through any attempt Maddie made at subterfuge. No, it was smarter to simply tell the truth from the start. "I need to talk to her about Mildred."

Instead of immediately responding, Marla blinked her eyes in rapid succession. "What are you talking about?" She looked confused enough that Maddie realized she was legitimately out of the loop.

"Your grandmother was tight with Mildred for a time," Maddie volunteered. "They were buddies. Er, well, the closest thing Mildred had to a buddy as far as I can tell. I need to ask her some questions."

"Grandma and Mildred were friends?" Marla didn't look convinced as she folded her arms over her chest. "I don't think that's true. I would know if they'd spent time together. Everyone has been talking about the girl you found for the past two days. I'm sure it would've come up."

"I would like to believe that's true," Maddie hedged. "The thing is, people remember a very specific time when Harriet and Mildred were hanging out together. I need to ask your grandmother about it."

When Marla didn't immediately give her an answer, Maddie pushed harder. "If I'm wrong about them being friends, she'll never let me hear the end of it. You can even be a witness to her dressing me down."

Marla brightened considerably. "Good point. Come on." She gestured for Maddie to follow her inside, not slowing until she reached a pretty sunroom at the back of the small ranch house. "Grandmother, you have a visitor."

Maddie didn't immediately see Harriet, but the moving shadow from a nearby rocking chair drew her attention. Maddie pasted a tight smile on her face when she saw the hateful look on Harriet's face, hoping against hope that Harriet's dislike for Maude wouldn't come back to bite the entire family now. "Hello, Mrs. Proctor."

"Oh, it's you." Harriet's voice practically dripped with disdain. "I should've expected you. Are you here to beg for me to drop the charges against Maude? If so, it's not going to happen. She's going to prison this time."

Maddie was understandably confused. "Why is Granny going to prison?"

"You saw my front lawn. That was her. I have proof and she's going to prison."

Maddie didn't believe that for a second. Even if Maude was caught vandalizing Harriet's lawn the worst she would get was community service. No judge would throw an elderly woman in the slammer for wasting toilet paper. "Well, I'll be sad not to see her on a regular basis, but since I can visit her in prison it's not a total loss."

Harriet narrowed her eyes to dangerous slits. "You're a little too upbeat for my liking, girl."

"That's what I always say," Marla lamented as she took a seat on the small wicker couch. "It's annoying, isn't it?"

Harriet ignored her granddaughter and remained focused on Maddie. "Why are you here? I assumed it was about Maude, but now I'm starting to think otherwise."

"I'm definitely here for a reason besides Granny," Maddie admitted, opting to sit in an uncomfortably rigid chair across from Harriet. "I'm here to ask you about Mildred Wilkins."

"I told her you weren't friends with Mildred because I would know about that," Marla volunteered. "She wouldn't believe me."

"She wouldn't believe you because it's not true." Harriet pursed her lips as Marla openly gaped. "I wondered if I would get a visit. I wasn't sure if anyone remembered that there was a time – however brief – where Mildred had my ear."

"I didn't know about it until someone mentioned it," Maddie hedged. "The thing is, my understanding is that Mildred might have been pregnant. She would've been around forty at the time and friends with you. Can you confirm that?"

"Why would you care if Mildred was pregnant?" Marla asked.

"Because they're trying to figure out who that girl they found belongs to," Harriet barked, annoyed. "That must mean you still haven't identified her."

"We know her name," Maddie countered. "It's Angel, in case you're wondering. Communication isn't exactly easy because she's deaf but she claims Mildred was her grandmother. We can't find a child on record for Mildred. However, someone swears up and down that Mildred appeared to be pregnant at one point about forty years ago. Do you know anything about that?"

Harriet calmly sipped iced tea and stared out the porch window for a long beat before answering. "The girl is deaf?"

Maddie knew she would have to give information to get information. She wasn't especially happy about it, but she didn't have a lot of options. "She is. She's going to be tested because we believe she can hear some sounds and might be able to be fitted for hearing aids. She can also read lips. I believe she can speak, but so far she's opted to communicate through sign language. It's slow going when asking questions."

"I see." Harriet tapped a wrinkled finger against her bottom lip. "Am I right in assuming that you believe Mildred gave birth and this child is really somehow her granddaughter?"

The question caught Maddie off guard. "I'm not sure what I believe," she admitted after some quiet contemplation. "I know that girl needs help. She's going to need a permanent placement and if she has a mother out there ... well ... we need to find her."

Harriet let loose a long-suffering sigh. "I don't want to help you on principle."

"You are going to help me, though, aren't you?" Maddie was certain that was true, although she had no idea why.

"I am." Harriet bobbed her head. "I'm doing it for the girl. Heck, maybe I'm even doing it for Mildred, although things didn't end well between us."

"Did she have a baby?"

Harriet shook her head. "She was faking being pregnant."

That wasn't the answer Maddie was expecting. "W-what? I don't understand."

"I'm not sure I do either." Harriet was resigned. "I just know that Mildred and I became friends because we both disliked Maude a great deal. We bonded because of it. I would never say we were especially close. We got along fairly well, though."

"And she faked a pregnancy?"

"She did." Harriet almost looked amused at the memory. "She told me she was going to do it. She said she didn't want me to talk about it because people would be more likely to remember she was pregnant if she acted like it wasn't a big deal, or maybe even that she was hiding it. That was all part of the plan."

What Harriet was saying made absolutely no sense to Maddie. "Are you sure she wasn't trying to fool you?"

"She stuffed her stomach with a pillow," Harriet replied. "I watched her do it practically every single day for two months."

"But ... why?"

"She wouldn't say. I honestly don't know why she wanted people to think she was pregnant. That's one of the reasons we fell out."

"Because you thought it was stupid to lie?"

"Because I wanted to know what Mildred was going to tell people when the time for her to give birth had come and gone," Harriet corrected. "I knew she had a plan and was doing something but, for the life of me, I couldn't figure out the endgame. That drove me crazy."

"I can see that." Maddie honestly understood Harriet's frustration. "What happened then?"

"Nothing." Harriet was matter of fact. "We had a fight because she wouldn't tell me what was going on. She basically cut me out of her life and never spoke to me again. She maintained the pregnancy ruse another month afterward and then she was suddenly thin again.

"I heard people in town ask what was going on with her – whether she had a baby or lost it – but I always said I didn't know because that was essentially the truth," she continued. "I always wondered if she was crazy and theorized about what she was plotting, but I never got proper answers to my questions. It looks like you're digging for the same answers now."

"Yeah." Maddie had no idea what to make of the story. "I don't understand why she would fake being pregnant."

"Join the club."

NICK WAS BURIED IN paperwork when he heard someone clear his throat near the door to his office. Even though he was annoyed at being bothered, Nick flicked his eyes in that direction and almost fell out of his chair when he recognized the man standing there. It was Steven Wilkins.

"I didn't know you were coming to town." Nick scrambled to get to his feet. "We were going to call to give you an update – I swear it – but I guess things fell through the cracks."

Steven looked more amused than offended. "That's okay." He held his hands up in a placating manner. "I don't want to bother you. I know you're busy and you're trying to put all this together. I got a call from the local funeral home, though. As Mildred's only relative, apparently I'm the one who needs to make decisions about her funeral."

Nick hadn't even thought of that. "Oh, wow. That's got to be rough." He gestured toward one of the open chairs across from his desk. "Have a seat."

"Thank you." Steven was obviously uncomfortable as he glanced around the small office. "I figured I should at least head over here to talk to the funeral home director. I don't know what insight I can offer – or if I should even be involved – but apparently there's no one else."

"There really is no one else," Nick confirmed. "We haven't found anyone on Mildred's family tree. I mean ... you're it."

Steven furrowed his brow. "That can't be right. I remember going to family reunions when I was a kid. I didn't have any cousins or anything – it was just Mildred and my father in their immediate family – but there were a lot of other relatives at the reunions. My father and Mildred had a lot of second cousins and the like."

"I'll look into that." Nick forced a smile that didn't make it all the way to his eyes. "You look tired."

Steven's smile was rueful. "So do you. I'm guessing you're tired because you're investigating my aunt's murder, though, and I'm merely tired of racking my brain for things that might be able to help you. I haven't been able to forget what you said."

"And what's that?"

"About the girl." Steven tapped his fingers on his knee as he jostled his foot, a restless gesture that Nick recognized as frustration. "I had nightmares last night. I kept picturing a little girl – and I have no idea what this one looks like so I made up a face in my head – and she was trapped and screaming as she tried to get out of the house. It was horrible."

"It wasn't quite that bad," Nick countered. "There was smoke in her room – I'm not going to lie about that – but she wasn't near the flames. Whoever set the fire clearly didn't know what he was doing because only the second floor was seriously damaged."

"That's good, right? That helps you."

"It does," Nick confirmed. "More importantly, general ineptness saved the girl and we have to be thankful for that."

"Can't you just ask her who she is?"

"We've been working on it." Nick wasn't sure how much information he should share with Steven. Ultimately, he decided holding back probably wasn't a good idea. "She's deaf."

"Deaf?" Steven's eyebrows hopped. "As in ... she can't hear or speak?"

Nick nodded. "We're still trying to ascertain if she can speak, but she hasn't yet so that leads me to believe she's incapable."

"Oh, wow." Steven's expression twisted. "That has to be even harder for you than I realized. You have a witness who can't communicate. Cripes. She just sits there and stares at a wall while you need answers about Mildred's death. That has to be so frustrating."

"I didn't say she couldn't communicate," Nick clarified. "She's deaf, but she knows sign language. We have an interpreter staying with her at all times and that allows for conversation. It was a rough first night, but it's gotten markedly better since then."

"Oh, really?" Steven brightened. "She's talking to people? That's good. What is she saying?"

"Oh, well, I can't go into that too much," Nick hedged. "I know it's difficult and you want answers – I can say without reservation that we all want that – but I have to protect the girl's privacy."

"I understand." Steven instantly turned contrite. "It's just ... I feel responsible for her."

"You shouldn't. This situation isn't your doing."

"No, but I've somehow been put in charge of my aunt's funeral," Steven explained. "I wasn't expecting that. For some reason, it was easier to put the situation out of my head until that happened. Then I got a call and ... well ... here I am."

"You don't have to take this on," Nick pointed out. "You didn't know her. You can back away and let whatever plans Mildred made stand."

"Except I don't know if she made plans. That's why I at least decided to drive over and have a meeting with the funeral director. I knew I would feel guilty if I didn't and ... well, I don't especially like feeling guilty."

"No one does," Nick conceded. "The thing is, you didn't know her and this isn't your responsibility. I understand wanting to do what you can because the guilt will eat you alive otherwise, but this seriously isn't your responsibility."

"Whether it is or not, I feel like it's my responsibility," Steven argued. "I need to do this. I won't be able to live with myself otherwise."

Nick considered pushing the issue further, but he knew it was a lost cause. If he were in the exact same position, he understood he would act the same way. "Well, let me know if you need anything. I don't know how much help I can offer."

"I'm actually thinking about staying here for at least a night," Steven admitted. "Can you point me toward a decent – and reasonable – hotel?"

"Oh, sure." Nick brightened. "The best one is right downtown. It's off-season so it won't be too expensive. It's about two blocks that way." He pointed for emphasis. "You can't miss it."

"Thanks."

"Also, if you're looking for dinner, there's a great diner on the main drag," Nick added. "My fiancée and I eat there several times a week. The food is really good. Like ... comfort food, if you know what I mean."

"I know exactly what you mean." Steven smiled. "I think I know where I will be eating dinner tonight."

"Have you been to the funeral home yet?"

"That's my next stop. I saw the police station and wanted to stop and see you. I thought maybe you would allow me to see the girl. I don't know why I want to see her but ... I guess I simply want to make sure she's okay."

"I wish I could, but I can't. She's under the care of CPS right now."

"Ah, right. I just thought maybe I might be able to recognize her or something, at least pick up on similarities if she belongs to other people in the family."

Nick was intrigued despite himself. "I never thought about that. It's a good idea, though. I'll bring it up to my contact with the state and see if we can arrange something."

Steven smiled. "Anything I can do to help. That's the most important thing to me. I want to be sure she ends up in a good place."

"We all want that. Trust me."

13. THIRTEEN

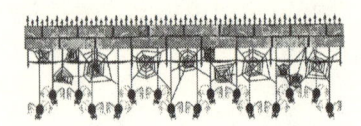

After another long day, Maddie and Nick opted for dinner at the diner. Maude was busy with her friends, casting a disdainful look over her shoulder when Nick asked her what they were plotting and then securely fastening her door rather than answering.

Maddie didn't care what her grandmother was up to. She figured plotting kept Maude young and she was all for that. She was also eager for someone else to do the cooking and after-dinner cleanup so she jumped when Nick suggested they head back to town. She had a lot of information to share – him, too – and it was easier to seclude themselves in their favorite booth than root through the refrigerator for something to cook.

"You guys are back again, huh?" Ruby smiled as she placed glasses of water in front of them. "Do you know what you want, or do you need more time?"

"I think we're going to need more time," Nick replied, inclining his head toward the door when the overhead bell jangled.

Maddie shifted her eyes in that direction and audibly gasped when she saw John and Christy standing there. They were doing their best not to look at one another and Maddie could practically feel the annoyance wafting off her friend. "That doesn't look good."

"It definitely doesn't," Nick agreed, raising his hand to get his brother's attention. "Let's see if we can help them fix it, huh?"

Maddie wasn't sure that was possible, but she readily agreed. "I didn't call Christy today because I was afraid she would yell at me." She moved to shuffle to one side so Christy and John could sit next to each other on the other end of the booth, but Christy stopped her from doing that by sliding in next to Maddie and forcing John to take the spot on the other side of Nick. That essentially meant Christy and John were separated from one another, but whenever one of them raised their eyes they would have no choice but to make eye contact.

Reading the heavy tone between the couple, Nick cleared his throat as he slung an arm over Maddie's shoulders and winked at Ruby. "Well, this is a nice surprise."

"Yes, it's positively lovely," Christy drawled, rolling her eyes.

Ruby licked her lips as she glanced between faces. "What can I get you to drink?"

"I'll have iced tea," Maddie replied immediately.

"That sounds good to me, too," Nick said.

"Make it three." John was morose as he snagged a menu from the center of the table. "If you have any bourbon in the back, throw a big shot of that in for taste, too, if you can manage."

Ruby's eyes twinkled as she turned to Christy. "And for you, honey?"

"Just water." Christy's voice was strained. "Apparently, now that I'm pregnant, I can't drink anything with caffeine." She focused on Maddie. "Did you know that was a thing? I certainly didn't. How am I supposed to go without caffeine for the next eight months?"

Maddie was unsure how to answer the question. "Oh, well, I was a nurse," she said. "I had to study things like that. I think you can have a glass of tea here or there. You simply can't have a pot of coffee to start each day."

Christy's eyes narrowed until they were nothing but glittery slits. "So, basically you're saying I can't do what I love."

"Oh, well ... ." Maddie broke off and chewed on her bottom lip.

Since he had Damsel in Distress Syndrome, Nick gave Maddie's shoulder a squeeze and opted to jump in and rescue her. "How did your appointment go earlier? What did you find out?"

"I found out that I can't have caffeine," Christy groused, staring hard at her menu.

"I see." Nick flicked his eyes to John. "What did you find out?"

John seemed more open to discussion, but he was clearly floundering because he constantly shifted as he tried to get comfortable in the booth. "She's six weeks along," John offered. "The baby is healthy, although Christy needs to take iron supplements and get a good night's sleep. Other than that, we just know that she's definitely pregnant and we'll be looking at a Christmas baby."

Maddie brightened considerably. "Really? That might be fun."

"Oh, sure." Christy sounded downright evil. "There's nothing better than a baby born at Christmas. That won't make the season uncomfortable or anything. I mean ... I can barely walk on the ice as it is."

"Well ... ." Maddie had no idea what to say to cheer up Christy. She'd never seen her friend this down. "It's still a baby. You have to be at least a little happy about that."

Nick was almost afraid to hear Christy's response, but when the energetic redhead raised her eyes he saw something else living in the depths of her tortured orbs. He was almost certain it was fear.

"I am kind of happy about having a baby," Christy hedged, making sure to avoid John's pointed stare as she folded her hands in her lap. "I've had some time to think about it and I'm not as upset as I was. Sure, I still have to get used to it, but it's not the end of the world."

"I never thought it was." Maddie patted her knee. "I'll help you. We can start planning a nursery. We can buy clothes. Oh, are you going to find out the sex of the baby beforehand?"

"We haven't decided yet." Christy finally shifted her gaze so she could pin John with a dark look. "We have a lot of things to discuss."

Nick didn't miss the chill settling over the table. As much as he didn't want to insert himself into whatever was going on between Christy and John, he felt a desperate need to ease the tension. "Does someone want to share with the class why you're looking at my brother as if he's Satan himself?"

"Not really," Christy muttered.

"Definitely not," John agreed.

Nick slid Maddie a sidelong look. "I don't suppose you could use your magic to read their minds, could you?"

Maddie was flabbergasted. "I don't have magic."

Nick was amused. "What would you call it?"

"I ... not magic." Maddie was adamant. "It's just a family trait that's been passed down for a few generations. It's a peculiarity. It's not magic."

Nick wasn't even remotely convinced. "If that's what you need to tell yourself, fine. I'm not in the mood to fight. I think we can only take one family fight at the moment. I'm still dying to know why these two will barely look at each other."

Even though she didn't consider herself a busybody by nature, Maddie was eager to figure out why John and Christy weren't the happiest people on the planet as well. Still, she wasn't comfortable invading her friend's mind. She'd never been able to do it at will anyway. It was always something that sort of happened. "Christy will tell us when she's ready."

"That will be never," John supplied. "We've agreed not to talk about it."

"No, *you* agreed not to talk about it," Christy snapped. "I merely gave in because I was hungry and was afraid I would starve to death at the rate we were going."

"You had two lunches today," John argued. "How can you possibly be hungry?"

Christy's eyes filled with fire as Maddie grabbed her arm to calm her.

"She's eating for two now, John," Maddie pointed out. "She needs food to sustain herself. You just said yourself that her iron is low."

"That doesn't mean she needs four meals a day," John muttered.

"And here we go." Christy was beside herself. "He thinks I'm going to get really fat and he's upset about it."

John rolled his eyes. "Oh, don't go there. I said nothing of the sort."

"He thinks I'm fat," Christy said. "In fact, do you know what he said at the doctor's office today? He asked the doctor if I was allowed to exercise while pregnant. Can you believe that?"

Maddie pursed her lips. "Well ... ."

"I asked him that because I was curious," John said. "If you need bed rest, then I want to make sure you get it. If it's better for you to get exercise, I want to make sure you get that, too. I don't know what to expect. This is new for me."

"Oh, really?" Christy drawled. "I thought you were an old pro."

"Okay, let's take a timeout here, huh?" Nick held up his hands to get everybody's attention, making a T to show he meant business. He was clearly at the end of his rope when it came to the fighting. "I don't understand why you guys are so worked up. You're having a baby. It's not as if we just got word that the nuclear holocaust is heading this way. What gives?"

"Ask your brother," Christy gritted out, folding her arms across her chest as she stared out into the sea of faces littered around the diner.

"I will." Nick kept his voice pleasant, but just barely. "John, would you like to tell me what's going on here? I thought after this afternoon you were going to make things better, not worse."

"I thought that, too." John rubbed at the back of his head as he sipped his water. "After our talk, I was feeling better. I wasn't as terrified as I was earlier."

"Why would you possibly be terrified?" Christy challenged. "I'm the one who has to push a bowling ball out of my body. I'm the one who has absolutely no idea if I'm doing this alone or with a partner. I'm the one who is going to get so fat you're going to be grossed out."

Maddie's heart pinched when Christy's eyes filled with tears. "I'm sure everything will be fine." She risked a glare at John as she rubbed her friend's back. "I can't believe you said that to her. I mean ... that's terrible."

"I didn't say that to her," John protested, his temper ratcheting up a notch. "She's making it up in her head."

"Oh, so now I'm crazy!" Christy threw up her hands in defeat. "I don't see how you manage to put up with me."

"See!" John extended a finger, frustration evident. "She makes things up in her head. I didn't say that."

"You did, too."

"Stop that right now," Nick hissed, forcing a smile when a few curious heads turned in their direction. "You're causing a scene. I don't like scenes. I want to know what happened today to completely derail both of you. It has to be something serious.

"When John left my office earlier, he was adamant about being a good father and doting on you, Christy," he continued. "He was looking forward to the doctor's appointment and at least half the fear he was feeling when he first stopped by had disappeared. So ... what gives?"

"I was looking forward to the doctor's appointment," John said. "What you said made sense. We're happy. Adding a baby to our lives isn't going to ruin anything like I initially worried."

Christy shifted her eyes to Maddie. "Can you believe him? He thinks I'm going to ruin his life."

"I don't think that's exactly what he said," Maddie hedged.

"You need to get your ears checked if you didn't hear him," Christy groused.

"And I think you need to take a chill pill," Nick shot back. "What did the doctor say about chill pills? Are you allowed to take those because I think you need an entire bottle right about now."

"Oh, well, good," Christy muttered, lifting her nose in the air. "I should've known you would take your brother's side. Men always stick together no matter how buttheaded they are."

Nick opened his mouth to say something harsh, but Maddie shook her head to cut him off. She understood that Christy was a mass of moods – fear, excitement, nervous energy, hope, and worry all warring for supremacy in her head – and if Nick picked a fight with her, she was liable to explode all over him.

"I don't think that's what Nick was doing." Maddie kept her voice low. "I get that you're upset and ... terrified." Maddie touched her hand to Christy's forehead and frowned. "Wow. You really are terrified, aren't you?" She knit her eyebrows. "I can feel it. You're afraid that you'll get fat and never lose the baby weight. You're afraid the baby will kill you when it comes out. You're afraid that John is more fun than you and the baby will like him better. Oh, and you're afraid that John doesn't love you and will run the first chance he gets. You poor thing."

Maddie threw her arms around Christy as the redhead burrowed her face into Maddie's hair. Nick and John exchanged a dumbfounded look, John being the first to speak.

"Did she just read her mind?"

Nick shrugged. "That's a very good question. I thought you said you couldn't do that, Mad."

"I didn't read her mind." Maddie refused to raise her voice even though her anger was growing with each passing moment. "I can't control it that way."

"I think you just did," Nick argued. "What else can you see in there? Can you see a way for John to make all this better?"

"I ... don't know." Maddie stroked Christy's head, her gaze momentarily falling on Marla across the way. She hadn't even seen her enter the diner. "What is Marla doing here again? Doesn't she know how to cook her own dinner?"

Nick bit back the urge to laugh. That was rich coming from her since this was their second night in a row at the diner, too. "I don't know." He watched as Marla said something flirty to her dinner companion. "She's with Steven Wilkins, though. That seems a bit ... odd."

"Who is Steven Wilkins?" John asked, thankful to be able to change the subject. "Am I supposed to know that name?"

"Mildred Wilkins' nephew," Nick supplied. "He stopped in the station earlier. He asked about a hotel. He must have found one ... and somehow ran into Marla."

"They look like they're on a date," Maddie noted as she rocked a sobbing Christy to offer comfort. "I shouldn't be surprised because Marla works fast but ... come on. That guy has been in town like three hours. She must have her skanky girl radar pointed at the town limits so she can get first dibs on newcomers."

Nick's eyebrows flew up his forehead as amusement washed over him. "Wow, Mad. That was catty. You've been ramping up the cattiness where Marla is concerned lately – which I admire – but that was a good one. I didn't know you could be that catty."

Maddie made a feral growling sound in the back of her throat but her smile told Nick she was teasing him. "Now you do."

"Yeah, well, I feel I should warn Steven about Marla, but he's a big boy," Nick said. "If he wants to hang out with her, that's certainly his business. I can't stop him. He doesn't have a lot of money, though. I'm not sure why Marla would be interested in him."

"Maybe she's interested in what she thinks he's about to inherit," Maddie countered. "I mean, as Mildred's only living relative, doesn't Steven get the house and contents?"

"True." Nick stroked his chin. "I don't think that house is worth all that much. Two hundred grand at the most."

"In this area, that's a lot of money to some people," Maddie noted. "He would probably get it all in the form of an insurance payout and land sale, too. That means cash. Marla might realize that."

"I guess." Nick leaned back in the booth and crossed his ankles. "I'll track Steven down tomorrow and give him a heads-up about Marla and her rascally ways. I'm not sure how he'll take it, but he's going through enough I don't want him to struggle with anything additional."

"That's probably not a bad idea."

"He asked to see Angel, by the way," Nick added. "He said he probably won't be able to recognize her, but there's always the chance that he might know who she belongs to if he sees her."

Maddie tilted her head, considering. "Do you think that's a good idea? Angel doesn't like men."

"I have no idea. I'm leaving it up to the social worker." Nick shifted his eyes to his brother, who appeared just about as unhappy as one person could possibly look as he watched Maddie console Christy. "Don't worry. I'm sure this is just hormones and whatnot. Things will get better."

"I don't see how they could get much worse," John grumbled.

"I agree," Christy sniffed. "He completely ruined things today."

"How did he do that?" Maddie was legitimately curious.

Christy jutted out her lower lip. "I don't want to say. It's totally embarrassing."

"I can't help fix it if you don't tell me what it is," Maddie prodded.

"I don't want anyone to know." Christy's voice cracked. "It's too embarrassing."

Amused despite himself, Nick pinned his brother with a mockingly severe look. "What did you do?"

"I was trying to be nice," John protested. "I thought she would think it was romantic."

"Oh, I'm almost afraid to hear this story," Nick said. "You didn't suggest some wacky sex thing, did you?"

"Of course not!"

"Then what was it?"

"Now I don't want to tell you." John folded his arms across his chest. "I think we should be done talking about this for the day."

"I think so, too," Christy said. "It's too embarrassing. It's the absolute worst thing that's ever happened to me."

"Oh, it can't be that bad." Maddie touched Christy's forehead again and her eyes went wide as she got a glimpse of the source of Christy's misery. When she turned on John, she was furious. "You proposed at the doctor's office?"

John's face went slack. "How did you know that?"

Maddie ignored the question. "You proposed while she was in stirrups and without a ring?"

"Oh, geez." Nick slapped his hand against his forehead. "Tell me that's not true."

"I was trying to do the right thing," John protested. "I wanted Christy to be happy. I thought marriage was the obvious next step. I mean ... we have two houses. We need one house ... and one bed to share ... and one baby room.

"You told me to figure out exactly what I wanted and that's what I did," he continued. "The second I figured it out, I thought Christy should know."

"But ... she was in stirrups, man." Nick was horrified on Christy's behalf. "Who taught you how to propose to a woman?"

"Hey." John turned belligerent. "We can't all be Mr. Romantic like you."

"I guess not." Nick fought hard not to laugh as he met Maddie's gaze. "I'll bet I'm looking really good to you right about now, huh?"

Maddie nodded without hesitation. "You have no idea."

"This is not my fault," John complained. "The world is conspiring against me."

"Yes, that must be it," Maddie said dryly. "It's everyone else and not you."

"It is."

"Whatever."

14. FOURTEEN

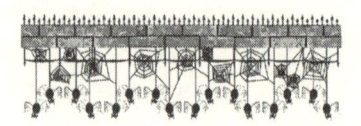

Nick woke early, although he couldn't immediately figure out why. Maddie was curled against him, as was her way, and she was clearly still in dreamland.

The morning light filtered through the window enough to allow Nick to glance around the room and when his eyes fell on his open door he found John standing there staring at him.

Nick barely managed to bite of a bitter curse and he held up a finger to keep John from saying something before carefully rolling away from Maddie. He was glad she opted to sleep in a tank top and shorts so she wasn't bare and exposed, but he tucked the covers around her anyway before padding toward the door.

He shoved John through the opening and directed him toward the stairs, running a hand through his hair as he descended.

"What are you doing?" he hissed when they hit the main floor. "How did you even get inside?"

"Maude." John's answer was simple. "I was going to wait until you guys got up, but Maude was doing something on the side of the house when I pulled up and she let me in."

Nick instantly turned suspicious. "What was she doing on the side of the house? I told her to get whatever she had hidden in that flowerbed out of there during our trip to Detroit. She promised she would because Maddie is intent on planting flowers this year and I don't want to have to arrest my future wife's grandmother."

"I have no idea what she was doing." John's eyes were red-rimmed, shadows dogging them as he heaved out a sigh and sank into one of the chairs Maddie had positioned around her small shop at the front of the house. "Does she ever get customers in here?"

"Some," Nick answered as he took the other chair. "I'm going to suggest closing the shop and just doing readings and stuff at festivals, but I haven't worked up to it yet."

"I can't imagine you would like having a store in your house."

"Well, as you've probably noticed, it's rarely open. The store was Olivia's baby, which is the only reason I think Maddie hasn't closed it yet. I don't get the feeling she likes running the store."

"If she closed it you could actually use this space for a living room, which is what it was designed for."

"I'm well aware what we could do with the space," Nick snapped. He wore nothing but his boxer shorts and his discomfort regarding John's appearance out of nowhere was obvious. "Now is not the time to bring it up to her. She's on edge. When you're dealing with a woman – this goes for all women, mind you – you have to pick the appropriate moment to spring something on them."

John groaned as he closed his eyes. "I knew you were going to bring that up."

"Please," Nick scoffed. "You're here at the crack of dawn because you need to talk. You were going to bring it up yourself."

"You don't know that."

"I know." Nick rolled his neck until it cracked. "Do you want to start with how stupid it was to propose when your girlfriend was in stirrups – and, for the love of everything holy, never describe the scene to me – or do you want to jump right to how you're going to fix it?"

"I honestly don't know." John's smile was rueful. "I didn't mean to do it the worst way imaginable. I really didn't. I just decided it was what I wanted ... and that it was probably what Christy needed ... so I did it. I didn't think about the ramifications until she was already screaming at me."

Nick's expression softened. "Believe it or not, I think you had her best interests at heart. Just out of curiosity, what did the doctor say?"

"Well, the doctor is a woman in her late forties. I'm sure you can guess how it went."

"She told Christy to dump you right then and there, didn't she?"

"Pretty much."

Nick snickered, genuinely amused. "Oh, geez. You always have to make things worse before you make them better, don't you?"

"Apparently that's my lot in life."

"Well, the good news for you is that I'm pretty sure you haven't screwed things up so badly that they can't be fixed," Nick noted. "The question is, do you want to fix them?"

John answered without hesitation. "Yes."

Nick was unconvinced. "You want to get married?"

"Yes."

"Are you sure you really want that?" Nick pressed. "Marriage is hard work. You have to want more than to make a family. You actually have to love Christy with your whole heart to make this work over the long haul."

"I'm not an idiot."

Nick arched an eyebrow.

"Okay, I'm not a complete and total idiot," John conceded. "I love her. When I picture my future, she's what I see. The baby is still like this fuzzy thing that I can't quite imagine, but I know the image will get clearer. Christy's image is already clear."

"That's good." Nick meant it. "I kind of figured that out myself, though. I was worried that you hadn't figured it out yet. You're ahead of the game."

"So, what do I do?" John leaned forward, plaintive. "She wouldn't even allow me into her house last night. I need to fix this. I was up all night, sick to my stomach. I didn't even want to drink."

"Oh, well, then it's definitely bad." Nick cracked a smile. "First off, you need to pick out a ring. You can't propose to someone without a ring."

"I don't even know what she likes, though."

"Luckily for you, I happen to know a blonde who does."

John stilled. "Oh. Do you think Maddie will help?"

"Of course I will," Maddie squealed from the staircase, her hair a mess of flaxen bedhead as she hurried down the stairs.

Nick smirked when he saw her, thankful she thought to put on a robe so her tiny pajamas weren't on display. "How long have you been listening? I tried not to wake you."

"I think it was your absence in bed that woke me," Maddie admitted, planting herself on Nick's lap so she could give John her full attention. She was beyond excited. "I'll go ring shopping with you. Wait ... let me feel out Christy first. She might actually tell me what her dream ring is and make this easy on us."

"Or you could just poke in her head," Nick suggested. "I'm going to bet, given what happened, everything you need to see is right there on the surface."

Maddie balked. "I already told you I can't do that at will."

"And yet I watched you do it last night," Nick argued. "Heck, I watched you do it twice in five minutes. I also think you've been doing it with Angel. I saw how you were with her the day of the fire. You were picking things out from her head."

"Emotions," Maddie corrected. "I didn't see anything that happened to her or anything. I just felt her emotions, what she was feeling, and it was overwhelming."

"Well, it seems to me that you should probably be able to direct that power if you really want to do it." Nick was pragmatic. "All it would take is some practice."

"I don't know." Maddie shifted on his lap. "I'll think about it."

"You do that." Nick smoothed her hair and turned back to John. "Maddie will help with the ring. That means all you have to do is come up with a romantic way to pop the question ... and I'm going to guess sooner will be better than later."

"Definitely." Maddie enthusiastically bobbed her head. "Almost all of Christy's fear is stemming from uncertainty and the biggest question mark in her life is you. She's afraid you don't really love her."

"That's ridiculous," John muttered. "How can she think that?"

"Have you ever told her you love her?" Nick asked.

"I ... well ... ."

"That's what I thought." Nick made a face. "How would she possibly know that you love her if you haven't told her?"

"Fine." John was exasperated. "I'll plan a romantic evening. I'll take her for a nice picnic, bring a bottle of wine along for the ride, and let nature take its course."

Maddie's eyes flashed with annoyance. "She's pregnant."

"I know."

"That means she can't drink."

John faltered. "Right. Crap. Maybe I should put together a plan and run it past you guys before enacting it, huh?"

"It couldn't hurt," Nick agreed, smirking. "I happen to think I'm a romantic soul so I won't steer you wrong."

"Nick is definitely a romantic soul," Maddie agreed. "Make sure he okays every step of your plan before you do something to make things worse."

"Way to prop up my ego, Maddie." John sent her a sarcastic thumbs-up.

Maddie was unbothered by his tone. "You should take her to that restaurant out on the lake, the one that is closed over winter. It's opening this week and she absolutely loves it. They have dancing, too, and Christy loves to dance."

John turned ashen. "Dance? I don't want to dance."

"It's not about you," Nick reminded him. "This is about Christy. Forget what you want and focus on her."

Maddie's gaze was keen as she shifted her eyes to Nick. "Is that why you haven't told me you would prefer I shut down the store so we can make a living room out of this space?"

Nick's mouth dropped open. "Were you just inside my head? If so, we're going to have to talk about that. Digging for a few things is fine. Constantly doing it is invasive."

Maddie rolled her eyes. "I wasn't in your head."

"Oh."

"I was eavesdropping at the top of the stairs."

Nick barked out a laugh. "I'm not sure that's better."

"You'll live." Maddie licked her lips as she glanced around. "I think you're right about the store, though. I don't think it belongs here. I loved my childhood and visiting my mother here was part of that, but I don't want our children to think of this place as anything but a home. If I want to have a store, it needs to move someplace else."

Nick was stunned how easy it was to convince her. "Are you sure?"

"Yes. I've been thinking it myself. I just need to talk to Mom first."

Nick rubbed her back. "I'm with you whatever you need."

John stared at them both, dumbfounded. "You guys are so good at this. I'm not sure I'll ever be as good at the love thing as you are."

"Give yourself time," Nick said. "You might be better than you think."

"Definitely." Maddie bobbed her head. "Now, who wants breakfast?"

Nick and John raised their hands in unison.

"I definitely saw that coming." Maddie hopped to her feet. "I'm thinking blueberry pancakes."

John's smile was so wide it overshadowed his face. "This is definitely the part of a relationship I could get used to."

"The part where the woman does the cooking?" Maddie challenged.

"The part where I get pancakes in the morning ... and a happy woman to eat them with."

Maddie grinned. "You're definitely getting better at this."

"That is the goal."

"I'M ABOUT TO BE your favorite grandmother," Maude

announced as she joined Nick and John at the table and expectantly looked at Maddie as her granddaughter toiled in front of the stove. "I want three pancakes this morning instead of two as my reward."

Maddie made enough pancakes to feed a small army so she wasn't particularly annoyed with her grandmother's demeanor as she carried a platter of pancakes to the table. "I only have one grandmother. I think you claimed that title a very long time ago."

"So cute." Maude grabbed Maddie's cheek and gave it a jiggle. "I guess that's why you're my favorite granddaughter, huh?"

"That must be it." Maddie whipped off her apron and sat in the chair between Nick and Maude. "Why are you my favorite grandmother today?"

"Because I have information about Mildred that is going to blow your investigation right out of the water."

"And how did you get that?" Nick asked.

"Beatrice Blythe."

Nick furrowed his brow. "Should I know that name?"

"She's a former Pink Lady who moved two towns over eight years ago and now only participates in special events on occasion."

"Oh, right. Beatrice Potter. She married some old guy and came into money, right?"

"You're so young." Maude made a tsking sound with her tongue. "That guy isn't all that old and he still has all his own teeth."

Nick grinned at Maddie. "Something to look forward to, huh, love?"

Maddie chuckled. "Yes. It's a lovely thing to endeavor toward. What's your gossip, Granny?"

"Well, it seems Beatrice got drunk with Mildred about ten years ago at one of the festivals," Maude explained. "Apparently it didn't take much. She said Mildred was a real lightweight."

"She should've joined the Pink Ladies and you would've taken care of that problem," John teased as he heaped syrup on his pancakes.

"You've got that right," Maude agreed. "When Mildred got drunk, though, she also got a case of loose lips and told Beatrice a rather fascinating story."

Even though Maude was prone to fits of exaggeration at times, Maddie felt the hair on the back of her neck stand on end. It was as if she knew she was about to learn something important.

"Well, don't keep us in suspense," Nick prodded. "What story did you hear?"

"It seems Mildred had a falling out with her brother."

Maddie's spirits sank. "We already know that, Granny. Her nephew told us the story."

"Did he tell you why they had a falling out?"

"I ... ." Nick broke off and searched his memory. "He didn't get into specifics. He said he couldn't remember why his father and aunt hated each other so much. It was just something that happened."

"Oh, it was definitely something that happened, but I have a hard time believing his father never told him the story." Maude rubbed her hands together, clearly relishing the story and her place in the spotlight. "It seems that Mildred's brother married her best friend shortly after Mildred and this woman – all I know is her name was Penny – graduated from high school."

Nick wrinkled his nose. "That can't be right. Steven said his father was a decent amount older than Mildred."

"No, that's part of the story," Maude said. "Apparently he started messing around with her when she was still illegal, but he didn't get into trouble because they got married right away."

"That's sick." Maddie put down her fork. "That's so wrong."

"Times were different back then and people got away with things," Maude supplied. "Anyway, she got pregnant right away and they had a child. It was a boy."

Nick did the math in his head. "No. Steven is in his forties. That math doesn't work."

Maude shot him a withering look. "Am I done yet?"

Nick held up his hands in mock surrender. "Sorry."

"Thank you." Maude rolled her eyes but continued. "They had a son who took off the minute he turned eighteen. His name was Edgar or something I think, although I can't really remember."

Nick filed away the tidbit for further research. "Okay."

"Apparently Mildred's brother was a real jerk and he mistreated Edgar and Penny a great deal. She was planning on leaving him when she got knocked up again. This was long after Edgar was already an adult."

"A late-in-life baby," Nick mused.

"Pretty much," Maude confirmed. "She was apparently pregnant – maybe very pregnant, although I'm not quite sure – when she approached Mildred for help to get away from the brother. Remember, this was forty years ago and domestic violence charges weren't taken as seriously."

Something niggled at the back of Maddie's brain, but she let it go.

"Mildred and Penny had a falling out when Penny married her brother," Maude volunteered. "Mildred warned her he was a jerk. Penny married him anyway. Blah, blah, blah. When Penny told Mildred what was happening, though, Mildred sprang into action and agreed to help."

"How did she help?" John was completely engaged in the story as he sipped his coffee.

"She helped Penny disappear."

"But ... how?" Nick asked.

Maude shrugged. "I don't know. I didn't get all the nitty-gritty details. All I know is that Mildred helped Penny disappear while pregnant with her second child and that the brother showed up and threatened to kill her if she didn't tell him where they were. Mildred refused to tell him and the cops were called, although no charges were filed."

Nick was dumbfounded. "I don't understand what you're saying," he said finally. "Are you saying that Angel is somehow tied to Penny?"

"I'm saying there was a lot more going on with that family than anyone realized," Maude corrected. "I don't know how it all sorts out – and Beatrice didn't either – but Mildred told her about it one day and said she didn't feel even a little bit sorry about it."

"I wouldn't feel sorry about it either," Maddie said. "If I were Mildred, I would've been proud. In fact, I'm kind of sad I didn't know about it before she died. I might have liked her a little better."

"I don't think she wanted anyone to like her because it made things easier when it came to keeping secrets," Maude supplied. "As for the girl Maddie found, I don't know how she plays into this. I'm going to guess that there's a convoluted story that needs unraveling at the center of it, though."

Nick was convinced she was right. "Well, at least I have somewhere to look when it comes to finding answers. I wonder why Steven didn't mention any of this to me?"

"Maybe he didn't know," John suggested.

"If Penny took him with her, though, how did he end up back with his father?" Maddie asked.

"That's a very good question, love." Nick forked a huge bite of pancakes into his mouth, swallowing before he continued. "I'm going to find out. I can promise you that."

15. FIFTEEN

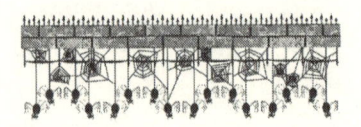

Nick knew exactly what Maddie was going to do with her day, although he didn't press her about it until he was dressed and they were standing in front of the main floor door.

"How are you going to find this woman if she's hidden?"

Maddie pursed her lips and shrugged. "What makes you think I'm going to do that?" She averted her eyes in an effort to be purposely evasive.

Nick snorted. "Because I know you. You're dying to know the true story behind Penny and Edgar. You also want to know how Steven fits into all this. You won't be able to stay away from it because your curiosity factor is off the charts."

Maddie thought about arguing, but it seemed like a waste of time. "I'm not sure how I'm going to find her," she conceded after a beat. "I have a few ideas, though. The question is, why aren't you trying to find her?"

"I am going to try and find her. Something tells me you're going to get to her first, though."

Maddie recognized his tone. "Do you not want me to find her?"

"I want you to remain safe," Nick clarified. "I know I can't stop you from looking."

"You really can't."

"Then be as safe as possible and message me throughout the day." Nick leaned forward and gave a quick kiss. "I love you."

"I love you, too." Maddie straightened his shirt collar. "I promise I'll be safe. You don't have to worry about me."

"I will always worry about you. I can't help myself."

"I know."

Nick opened the door. "Stay away from Mildred's house. I don't care how you find this woman but stay away from the house. You're exposed up there and I don't want to risk it."

"I have no intention of going to the house."

Nick was honestly curious how Maddie expected to track down a woman with no last name, but he decided to press Maddie on her efforts later. "I'll keep in touch, too. If I have any information, you'll be the first to know."

"That sounds like a plan."

MADDIE WAVED FROM THE front window until Nick was clear of the driveway and then immediately headed toward her grandmother's apartment. She didn't bother to knock and Maude's annoyance was evident when Maddie strolled in and caught her with a fresh batch of toilet paper.

"I believe you've been taught proper etiquette," Maude chirped. "You're supposed to knock when entering someone's home."

"You'll live." Maddie was blasé. "Tell me what you were holding back over breakfast."

Maude furrowed her brow. "What are you talking about?"

"You know more than you were saying." Maddie refused to back down. "I saw the way you were shifting on your chair when John and Nick asked a few rather pointed questions. I think you know where Penny is."

"Well, I don't."

Maddie wasn't about to be shut down. "Then I think you know

where she was ... at least at one time," she said. "If Mildred had loose lips, I'm going to assume that included a location."

Maude sighed, annoyance evident. "I might have an idea."

"Well, I need you to share that idea." Maddie was firm. "I need to track down Penny if she's still alive."

"Why?"

"Because Angel has to belong to someone. Mildred couldn't have been the only one who knew who she was. If Mildred helped Penny once before, maybe Angel is actually tied to Penny and Mildred was trying to help a second time."

Maude's eyes gleamed. "I didn't even think about that."

"So, where is she?"

"Not far." Maude brightened considerably. "She's a lot closer than I would've expected but maybe that's for the best. She was essentially hiding in plain sight."

"Give me what you've got."

PENNY WILKINS WAS NOW GOING by the name of Priscilla Grimes. She lived one town over in a pretty ranch house with gorgeous gardens and she seemed resigned more than surprised when she found Maddie on her front porch.

"I knew this would happen." She pushed open the door so Maddie could enter. "What took you so long?"

Maddie tried not to take the comment as an insult. "Do you know who I am?"

"I saw you on the television," Priscilla replied, pointing toward the kitchen and prodding Maddie to walk in that direction. She was older – Maude's age – but she was surprisingly spry. "I recognized Mildred's house. The police tried to shield you from the cameras – or maybe they were trying to shield the girl, I don't know – but your face isn't easy to forget."

"Oh, well ... ."

"Sit down." Priscilla pointed toward the kitchen table. "I just finished brewing a pot of coffee. We're probably going to need refreshments if this conversation takes the turn I expect it to."

Even though she was curious and wanted to start lobbing questions at Priscilla, Maddie managed to hold it together until the elderly woman returned to the table with the coffee.

"So, you're Maude Graves' granddaughter, huh?" Priscilla made a clucking sound with her tongue as she shook her head. "You don't look a thing like her."

"I've heard that a few times," Maddie admitted before sipping her coffee. Now that she'd actually found the woman – and it was easier than she anticipated – she had no idea what to say to her.

"I'm guessing you heard a story or two," Priscilla noted, her smile enigmatic. "How much do you want to know?"

Was that a trick question? Maddie couldn't be sure. "I want to know all of it," she said finally. "I want to know about your husband ... and Edgar ... and Steven. I want to know absolutely all of it."

"Then I guess I'll start from the beginning, huh?" Priscilla sipped her coffee and sucked in a cleansing breath. "I married Steven Wilkins shortly after high school. I thought he was smart and sophisticated because I was still underage when we hooked up and I didn't know any better. I was young and dumb so I fell for his act.

"A lot of people told me not to marry him – Mildred being one of them – but I refused to listen," she continued. "Back in those days we didn't have a lot of choices. It was marry and start a family or risk trying to become a career woman and spend your entire life struggling. You have a lot more choices now, and I envy you for them."

"I never really thought about it that way, but it makes sense," Maddie admitted.

"We were only married two weeks when he hit me for the first time," Priscilla volunteered. "At first it was slaps here and there, the occasional kick. I went to my mother and told her what was going on. I thought she would do something ... or at least know something I was supposed to do. She told me that was how marriage worked and I had to suck it up."

Maddie's stomach twisted. "I'm sorry."

"I am, too, but it's not like I wasn't warned." Priscilla was a pragmatic soul and she merely shook her head at the memory. "I was ready to leave Steven – I honestly didn't care how things went for me, but I knew it was no longer a tolerable situation – but I turned up pregnant and then I knew I was in a whole heap of trouble.

"I had no way of raising a child without help and Steven was so excited when I told him that I was expecting," she continued. "He didn't touch me for the entire duration of the pregnancy and I thought he'd seen the error of his ways.

"I found out that was not true two weeks after giving birth," she said. "He went right back to his previous self and things were actually worse after that. The only thing I had going for me was that he didn't touch Edgar. He seemed to revere the baby."

Maddie could already see where the story was going. "How long did that last?"

"Until Edgar was five and started mouthing off to him occasionally," Priscilla replied ruefully. "Edgar was a smart child and figured out how to survive at a young age. He played up to his father's sense of ego and that worked until Edgar was a teenager.

"After that, things were more ... difficult," she continued. "Edgar outgrew Steven when he was fifteen. He was still too frightened to raise a hand against his father, but by the time he hit seventeen he was ready for a fight. The next time Steven tried to go after him he put him on his behind."

Maddie smiled as Priscilla's face flushed with pleasure. She was clearly enjoying the memory.

"Edgar left right away when he was eighteen," Priscilla said. "He basically ignored his father's existence after that, although we were still close. He didn't go to college, but he started his own landscaping business and does quite well today."

A name clicked into place in Maddie's head. "Edgar Grimes Landscaping."

Priscilla brightened. "Do you know him?"

Maddie shook her head. "Not personally. I know a few people he works for, though. He has a very good reputation."

"He does." Priscilla preened under the compliment. "He's been married to the same woman since he was twenty-three. He has grown children of his own now. I'm happy to say he's ten times the father and husband Steven was. The apple fell far from the tree on that one."

"I'm glad." Maddie meant it. "You stayed with him after your son graduated and left the house, though. Why?"

"By then he was older. He was still just as mean, though. He was constantly yelling, but he was so drunk most of the time he passed out in the middle of the afternoon most days so it was easy to get past him."

Maddie couldn't imagine living that sort of life. "Something changed, though."

Priscilla bobbed her head. "I got pregnant again."

"You were older this time, though, right?"

"I was," Priscilla agreed. "I was in my forties. Granted, it was my early forties, but I was still older. I thought I was well past my child-bearing years."

"I guess not."

"No. When I visited the doctor, I thought something might be wrong ... like cancer maybe," Priscilla explained. "When he told me I was pregnant, well, you could've knocked me over with a feather.

"At first I was unhappy, terrified even," she continued. "I didn't want to raise another child because I didn't think I had the energy. Then, when I gave it more thought, I knew I didn't want to raise a child with Steven because I was convinced I wouldn't be able to keep a second child safe."

"That's when you left him," Maddie noted.

"Yes. I was pregnant – several months along – and I contacted Mildred for the first time since right after I got married," Priscilla confirmed. "I'd seen her at various family functions over the years, mind you, but she was always cold and wanted nothing to do with me. I think part of her was angry because I didn't listen to her."

"Well, she should've gotten over that sooner," Maddie argued. "You were the one who paid for it."

"I'm not sure she knew that. Anyway, it ultimately didn't matter. I reconnected with Mildred and told her my predicament. She wasn't surprised, but she didn't do that 'I told you so' thing I was expecting either. She was very matter of fact and eager to help."

"How did you do it?" Maddie was legitimately curious.

"It wasn't as difficult as you might imagine," Priscilla replied. "You need to remember, that was in a time before everyone had a computer, cell phone and access to Google. Disappearing back then was easy ... and I only moved two towns away to do it."

"I guess that makes sense." Maddie leaned back in her chair. "This would've been about the same time Mildred was faking being pregnant, right? How does that play into everything?"

Priscilla's smile was rueful. "Oh, you heard about that, huh?" She let loose a hollow laugh that was completely and totally humorless. "So, the plan was to give up the baby for adoption. I know you probably think that's terrible, but I thought it was for the best."

"I don't think it's terrible," Maddie argued. "I can see why you made that decision."

"The plan was for Mildred to pretend to be pregnant and hand over the baby when it was time," Priscilla explained. "When it came time to flee from Steven, it wasn't difficult at all. He went to work one day, Mildred showed up five minutes later, we packed all my stuff and were out of there before lunch. It was a lot easier than I thought it would be."

"Did you ever see Steven again?"

"Unfortunately, yes. I saw him from afar a time or two. Each instance was terrifying, but he didn't see me."

"That's good."

"It was ... a relief." Priscilla sipped again. "I didn't want him knowing I was pregnant. Even back in those days we had to worry about paper trails. I didn't want him getting his hands on the baby even though I was convinced I didn't want another child.

"So, like I said, the plan was for Mildred to pretend she was pregnant so she would be the one to fill out the adoption paperwork," she continued. "Her husband was barely around – he had a bunch of different girlfriends and didn't care about anything Mildred did – and she shoved pillows under her dress to sell the ruse. We didn't need it to be really convincing, just convincing enough to start up some gossip so Steven wouldn't question who the baby belonged to if he heard the story."

"The plan fell apart, though," Maddie noted. "Something happened."

"I went into labor and had a baby. Once I saw him ... I couldn't give him up. I told Mildred about my decision. I thought she would fight me when I told her I'd changed my mind. She was fine, though. She said no one would be brave enough to ask why she was faking being pregnant and not to worry about it."

"So what happened after that?"

Priscilla shrugged. "I raised my son."

"Why did you name him after Steven?"

Priscilla frowned. "I didn't. He chose that name himself after ... well, after he found out the truth. You see, he didn't have it easy growing up. People made fun of him for not having a father. I told him his father died – a story he believed – but ultimately he found out the truth."

"Was his father still alive then?"

"Yes. Not for long, but yes. Steven was in the hospital when he and Michael – that's what I named him – first connected. Michael spent weeks with him, sitting diligently at his bedside, and Steven spun some tall tales. By then he wasn't a threat because he was weak and dying. Michael believed the stories even though Edgar and I tried to make him see the truth."

Maddie's heart went out to the woman. "So Michael purposely took his father's name?"

"That was Steven's idea." Priscilla scowled. "He left Michael a little bit of money – not much, mind you, but enough for a young man to be tempted – but he really wanted someone to carry on his name. Michael acquiesced and that's how Steven Wilkins, Jr. was born."

Maddie found herself more sympathetic than horrified. "It must have been hard on him."

"It was," Priscilla agreed. "He was a good boy who thought he knew the story of his life and then found out his mother was a liar. It didn't go over well with him. He's still a good boy, though. He simply doesn't know the true story of his father and the lies Steven told him seem to have turned him bitter."

"Well, maybe he'll outgrow his resentment eventually."

"I don't think that's going to happen. Still, Steven is dead. He can't twist Michael's mind. That's the most important thing."

"Why didn't you come forward when Mildred died?" Maddie asked. "I mean ... you could've filled in a few blanks here and there."

"Because I put Penny Wilkins behind me and didn't want to show up in a bunch of police reports," Priscilla replied without hesitation. "I know it was wrong but ... I didn't think it would be a big deal."

"And what about the girl we found in Mildred's house?" Maddie questioned. "Who is she?"

"I don't have an answer for you. No, honestly, I don't." Priscilla's expression was earnest. "I have no idea who she is or why Mildred had her. If I knew, I would've come forward no matter how uncomfortable it was for me. I'm not a heartless monster. I'm simply ... careful ... with my former identity."

Maddie understood that, of course, but she persisted nonetheless. "There has to be a way to track down who that girl is and where she came from. She can't simply have materialized out of nothing."

"I don't know what to tell you." Priscilla absently patted Maddie's hand as it rested flat on the table. "I guess I can ask around, but I don't know anyone still alive, someone who knew Mildred well, who might have answers."

"Yeah." Maddie rubbed the back of her neck, frowning when her phone started to ring. "I'm sorry. I need to grab this." She tugged out the phone and frowned when she saw Nick's name pop up. She hit the "accept" button on the screen and worked hard to make sure her irritation wasn't obvious. "Hello?"

Nick didn't bother with greeting her. "Maddie, you have to get to the children's home right away."

Maddie was instantly on her feet. "What happened? Did something happen to Angel?"

"Love, I don't know the whole story yet," Nick cautioned. "I know that someone tried to visit Angel at the children's home and she freaked out. She's under the bed and hiding. We need you to help get her out. Sharon called me trying to find you. That's how desperate she is."

Maddie swallowed hard. "I'm on my way." She disconnected and forced a smile for Priscilla's benefit. "Thank you for explaining things to me. I have to get going."

"Is everything all right?" Priscilla asked. "You look white as a ghost."

"I don't know." Maddie shoved her phone in her pocket. "I have to go, though. Thank you so much for your time."

16. SIXTEEN

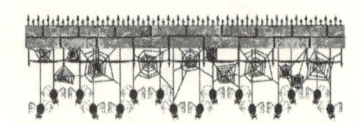

Nick paced the front lobby of the children's home waiting for Maddie to arrive. Sharon watched him, her mind busy.

"How long do you think it will take her?"

Nick shrugged. "She was coming from Bellaire. It shouldn't take her more than forty minutes." He checked his watch. "That means she's probably only a few minutes out."

"I hate having to call her but ... well ... Angel only seems to really perk up when she sees Maddie and she's a screaming mess right now."

"I'll have to take your word for it." Nick was grim. "She didn't like me from the start. Maddie will go in there and calm her down."

"You seem to have tremendous faith in her."

"I believe Maddie can do anything she sets her mind to," Nick said. "She's ... magic."

Sharon's expression turned rueful. "You love her."

"More than anything," Nick agreed, striding to the door and pulling it open just as Maddie appeared on the other side of the threshold. Her face was flushed and she was breathless, although she didn't let that stop her as she hit the lobby. "You made good time."

"I might have broken a few speeding laws on my way," Maddie admitted. "Don't give me grief about it."

"I'll issue some personal citations when we're alone later." Nick forced a smile as he took Maddie's hoodie. "Did you find what you were looking for this morning?"

"As a matter of fact, I did." Maddie didn't return the smile. "I got the whole story ... and it's interesting ... but it can wait until after I see Angel. Is she in her room?"

Sharon nodded. "She is. She's no longer under the bed but she's hiding in the corner. She doesn't want to see anyone. She doesn't want to talk to anyone. That's why we thought you might be able to help. She always perks up when you come to visit."

"I'll do my best." Maddie was determined as she walked through the building. "I still don't know what happened, though. You said someone came to see her. Who was it?"

"I have no idea," Nick replied, his expression turning sour. "The cameras on the front door are wireless and someone managed to blank the system at the exact time our visitor showed up."

"Someone had to talk to him," Maddie argued. "There's no way he walked into this building without anyone noticing."

"Oh, well, that's kind of what he did do." Sharon shifted from one foot to the other, uncomfortable. "He walked through the front door and didn't say a word to anyone. The woman at the front desk assumed he was here for a reason – that he knew where he was supposed to be – and didn't say a word."

Maddie was incensed. "How can that be possible? This is a children's home. There have to be security procedures."

"And he bypassed most of them," Sharon admitted. "He slipped through the cracks. I don't know what else to say."

"Did he see Angel?"

"Through the observation glass. Her door was locked, which I'm thankful for, and he tried to talk to her. I don't think he realized that she couldn't see him. She heard him, though, and that's when she started freaking out."

Maddie's stomach twisted. "What did he say to her?"

"My understanding is that he simply said normal things, like he was going to take her home," Sharon replied. "He acted like her father."

Maddie was intrigued ... and furious. "How did Angel hear him if he was on the other side of the glass?"

"I ... ." Sharon broke off, puzzled. "That's a very good question. I honestly don't know. We had her hearing tested yesterday afternoon and the results were inconclusive. The doctor said she thought Angel heard more than she indicated but had no proof of it. We were going to have a specialist come and see her this afternoon, but apparently that's not going to happen as long as she's acting this way."

"Why would she fake how well she can hear?" Nick was legitimately curious. "How could that possibly benefit her?"

"I don't know," Maddie answered. "I think it's more important to figure out who was here, though. Someone must have an idea. Someone should be able to describe him to you."

"I'm on it, Mad." Nick tried not to take offense at Maddie's tone. "I wanted to make sure you got here safely first. I'm going to ask some questions, although this isn't technically my jurisdiction. I have to clear it with area law enforcement first."

Maddie wasn't even remotely placated. "Figure out who it is. I'm not kidding. If he managed to scare Angel, that means he's not a good person. I don't want him in here again."

"We're increasing security on the entire building for at least the next few days," Sharon offered. "We're going to have an officer positioned here twenty-four hours a day. It won't happen again."

"Make sure it doesn't." Maddie took a deep breath outside Angel's room and pasted a bright smile on her face before entering. She didn't look over her shoulder to see if Sharon was insulted by her order. She honestly didn't care. "Hello, sweetheart," she called out. "How are you?"

Nick watched through the window as Maddie sat on the bed rather than crowded the girl. She kept up a steady stream of chatter but refrained from forcing Angel to interact with her.

"That's smart," Sharon said as she moved to stand next to Nick.

"She's not forcing Angel to do anything she doesn't want to do and instead is building up a blanket of trust. I'm impressed."

Nick didn't immediately respond, his eyes focused on Maddie as she talked to a girl who refused to acknowledge her existence.

"Has Maddie ever considered being a social worker?" Sharon asked. "She might be good at it."

"I have the greatest respect there is for social workers," Nick supplied. "I think the job you guys do is important and harder than pretty much any other job out there."

"But?" Sharon prodded.

"But doing this job would kill Maddie's soul and I have no intention of ever letting that happen," Nick replied honestly. "Dealing with abused children would break her. She's not geared toward this type of work."

"And what type of work is she geared for?" Sharon asked. "I did a little research on her and found she owns a magic shop. That doesn't seem like a good way to make a living ... or is that not important because you take care of her?"

Nick scowled, his temper firing. "You don't know anything about Maddie. She's a hard worker. She gives of herself constantly. The magic shop belonged to her mother. It's not her baby."

"And where is her mother?"

"Dead."

"Oh." Sharon was taken aback. "I didn't mean to insult her or anything."

"That's exactly what you intended to do," Nick countered. "You were digging for information. I get it, by the way. Maddie is often an enigma and people can't help being curious about her. It doesn't matter what she does for a living, though. It matters who she is as a person. And, for the record, she's the best person I've ever known."

"I honestly wasn't casting stones or anything. I just ... she could be good at this."

"Doing something like this would be bad for her, though," Nick argued. "You've seen how attached she is to Angel. Now imagine she has sixty kids on a list she's supposed to watch out for. It would kill her."

"Or be the best thing that ever happened to her."

Nick vehemently shook his head. "No. I've known her since we were five years old. This would kill her."

Sharon heaved out a sigh as she watched Maddie fruitlessly try to engage Angel through the window. "It was just a suggestion. She's very good with Angel."

"Maddie won't stop until she's sure Angel is safe," Nick said. "She'll die to make sure it happens. That is not the basis of a good social worker. That is the basis of a good person, though."

"Maddie is the best person I've ever known," he continued. "I have no idea what she's going to do with her life – other than marry me and live happily ever after – but I know it's not going to be this. This world would chew her up and spit her out. I think she's going to have to make her own working world down the line ... and I'm looking forward to seeing where her imagination takes her."

Something about Nick's tone stirred Sharon. "I guess you know best."

"When it comes to this, I do," Nick agreed, forcing himself to turn away from the window. "We need a description of the man who was here. Maddie is going to be in there for a decent amount of time. We should get to the work out here."

"Sure." Sharon bobbed her head. "Where do you want to start?"

"The main secretary. I want to know exactly what she saw."

"Then let's start there."

NICKI AND MADDIE WERE both so exhausted by the time they returned to Blackstone Bay that they headed straight to the diner for dinner. Nick recognized Maddie was bone tired – Angel refused to speak or even acknowledge her existence despite three hours of hard work – and he knew they would both want nothing more than to tumble into bed and sleep when they returned home.

"This is starting to be a habit," Ruby said once they were settled.

"I can't remember the last time you guys were in here three nights in a row."

"Yes, well, we're tired." Nick lightly rubbed Maddie's back as he glanced at the specials menu. "Oh, you guys have prime rib tonight. That sounds really good. I'll have that with mashed potatoes and whatever the house vegetable is."

Ruby turned to Maddie. "And you, sugar?"

"That sounds good to me, too." In truth, Maddie wasn't overly hungry, but she knew Nick would put up a fight if she tried to skip dinner. At least this way he could have her leftovers for a treat. "I'll have the same thing."

"You got it." Ruby winked at Nick before leaving. It was clear she sensed Maddie's distress, but she wasn't the type to pry.

Nick waited until he was sure Ruby was out of earshot to speak again. "You can't let this depress you, Mad. You did the best you could."

"She wouldn't even look at me. It was as if she was in her own little world."

"Maybe she was." Nick had trouble wrapping his mind around Angel's hearing issue and he needed someone to break it down with. Maddie was the obvious choice. "What if she can hear?"

Maddie rolled her eyes. "If she could hear, why does she need sign language?"

Nick shrugged. "Maybe she can't speak. Maybe it's not her hearing that's an issue but, for whatever reason, she simply can't speak."

Maddie stilled. That possibility hadn't even occurred to her. "But ... how would that happen?"

"I honestly don't know. I have trouble believing someone with limited hearing range could make out a voice on the other side of the observation window, though. I tested it in another room while you were busy with Angel. They have two with observation windows."

"And?"

"And the man wasn't yelling," Nick replied. "He used a booming voice – at least that's what the witness said – but he wasn't yelling. I tested it with Sharon. She yelled fairly loudly, and it was muffled. If Angel really can't hear, how would she be able to make that out?"

He had a point. Maddie didn't want to admit it, but some of what he said made sense. "Maybe she can hear." Maddie worked her jaw as Ruby delivered iced tea to the table, her mind busy. "What could cause someone not to be able to speak?"

"Well, I did some research while you were in with Angel." Nick dug his phone out of his pocket and pulled up the notes he'd taken. "There are several types of muteness. The first is selective muteness, which is a form of anxiety that often affects children. If Angel was traumatized, it might not be that she physically can't speak, but she somehow chooses not to."

Maddie didn't like that idea one bit. "But ... if it's voluntary, why go through the trouble of teaching her sign language? It seems to me that a parent would rather wait something like that out."

"I had the same thought," Nick admitted. "There's Alalia, which results in speaking delays in children. Sometimes it's never corrected. There's Aphasia, which can rob all aspects of speech and often accompanies a head injury.

"There's Aphonia, which is when people can't produce any voice," he continued. "There are also several forms of Autism and conversion disorders. That's on top of physical reasons. Damage to the esophagus, vocal cords, lungs and mouth can cause muteness. However, she can scream – we've heard her scream multiple times – and I don't think it's a problem with her vocal cords. There's honestly a lot of different reasons why someone might not be able to talk, though, and I'm not sure which one we're looking at."

Maddie rubbed her forehead, weariness overtaking her. "If I had to guess, I would think something happened to her. She's terrified for a reason. Someone did this to her."

"I would agree, but we need a medical diagnosis to prove that," Nick cautioned. "That means we need a doctor to look her over and she's not going to allow that anytime soon."

"No," Maddie agreed, resigned. "The hearing thing never honestly made sense. I know she heard me the day I saved her. I yelled through the window. It was one of those wavy ones that distorts the view so there's no way she read my lips. I told her to duck and cover and she did.

"After that I kind of forgot that part," she continued. "I just assumed when she started signing that she was deaf. That wasn't the right way to go."

"Oh, don't do that." Nick wagged his finger. "I don't want you blaming yourself. You're the only reason she's safe. If you hadn't found her when you did, something terrible might've happened in that house."

"You're assuming something terrible didn't happen in that house."

"No, I'm not." Nick was matter of fact. "I have been slowly coming up with a theory, though. I have no way to prove it, but I think I might know what happened."

Maddie widened her eyes, officially intrigued. "Tell me."

"First, tell me how your meeting with Penny went," Nick instructed. "I want to see if your facts fit my theory before going forward."

"Okay." Maddie wasn't keen to wait for information but she understood it was important to Nick's process. "It's a long and convoluted story."

"I'm fine with that."

Maddie launched into her tale. By the time she was done, their dinner was served and Maddie had managed to mow through half of the huge prime rib helping. Apparently she was hungrier than she thought.

"So, that's basically it," Maddie said when wrapping up. "Michael changed his name to Steven and he embraced a jerk of a father. His mother makes excuses for him – she tried to pretend otherwise, but I could see that's what she was doing – and now he's living off the money his father left him."

"Huh." Nick stroked his chin, his expression unreadable. "That's not exactly the story I remember from our first meeting."

Now it was Maddie's turn to be interested. "Really? How was his story different?"

"He mentioned going to family reunions with his father and he knew all about Mildred's feud with her brother. I assumed he spent a lot of time with his father. The story Penny told you is vastly different."

"What are you getting at?"

Nick shrugged. "Is it possible she was lying?"

Maddie immediately started shaking her head. "I know you're probably going to laugh at this, but she wasn't lying. Her story was true. I ... felt it."

"Well, that's good enough for me. That means Steven was lying."

Maddie thought back on her earlier conversation with Priscilla. "She doesn't go by Penny any longer, by the way. It's Priscilla."

"Okay."

"She wasn't lying to me." Maddie was firm on that. "I'm not sure she told me everything, though. At the time, I thought maybe she was simply avoiding things in her story that she was embarrassed to share."

"And now you're not so sure?"

"I honestly don't know," Maddie replied. "I definitely think there's more to the story."

Nick flicked his eyes to the front door when the overhead bell jangled, making an odd noise in the back of his throat when Marla and Steven walked in together. "Well, look at that. It's almost as if he knew we were talking about him."

Maddie followed his gaze. "What is he doing with Marla?"

"Maybe they're dating."

"He's been in town less than forty-eight hours."

"Hey, Marla moves fast." Nick wrinkled his forehead as he regarded the duo. "Maybe I should go over there and ask him about the new development. I'm curious if he would be able to explain away the things his mother said to us. I'm guessing it wouldn't be all that easy given what he's already told us."

"Don't do that," Maddie argued. "At least ... not yet. If Steven knows his mother is talking out of turn, it might set him off. I have a better idea."

Nick sawed his prime rib and slid Maddie a curious look. "You have an idea? Do I even want to know what it is?"

"Probably not." The smile Maddie mustered was genuine. "I still think it's what we should do."

Nick thought about arguing, but the twinkle in her eye forced him to make another choice. "Fine. What is your idea?"

"It's a good one. I promise."

Nick had his doubts. "Lay it on me."

17. SEVENTEEN

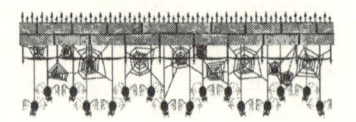

"**T**his is ridiculous." Maddie and Nick returned home long enough to drop off her car and head straight back to the diner. Maddie looked through the eatery's window and ascertained Marla and Steven were still inside before hopping inside Nick's truck and hunkering down to wait.

It wasn't long before Nick made his feelings known.

"If you don't want to spy, you don't have to." Maddie adopted a prim tone. "You can leave your truck with me and walk home. I'll do the spying on my own. I simply thought it was something we could do together, but if you're too adult for it ... well, you don't have to stay. I'm fine being alone."

"Oh, geez." Nick slouched down in the driver's seat, showing no signs he was going to do as Maddie suggested. "Like I'm really going to leave you to carry out a covert operation on your own. That's not going to happen."

"Then stop complaining."

Nick slid her a sidelong look. Her cheeks were flushed with color, her gaze intense, and she looked from all outward appearances as if she was actually enjoying the mission. Since he'd been on more surveillance trips than he wanted to admit – especially during his training and academy days – Nick was a more reluctant participant. "Can I ask you something?"

"Yes, I love you more than anything."

Nick didn't want to laugh at her response – it would only encourage her, after all – but he couldn't stop himself. "I love you more than anything, too. That's not what I was going to ask, though."

Maddie let loose a long-suffering sigh. "Fine. I guess if we're going to be partners you've earned the right to ask questions."

"Oh, well, thank you for allowing it." Nick poked her side so she would know he was teasing. "What do you expect to discover from this, Mad? I mean ... what do you think is going to happen between Steven and Marla tonight?"

"I honestly have no idea." Maddie saw no reason to lie. "The thing is, Marla wanted in on the action the other day. She was questioning us because she wanted answers. Now, I don't think she wanted to offer her services for altruistic reasons or anything. It was more that she was bitter about not being in on the action.

"If we're right about Steven and he's up to something – I really think you should take a photograph of him back to the children's home tomorrow, by the way, just to be sure – then maybe he's good at reading people," she continued. "Marla hops on any new man within a certain age range whenever he crosses the town line. Maybe she did that with Steven and he realized she might be useful."

"Or maybe he just wants to get some and figured Marla was primed to give it up," Nick countered. "We both know how Marla is. She's not the type to make someone play the long game. Steven could simply want some company."

"Sure. That's possible."

"So, why are we spying on them again?"

"Because I have a feeling." Maddie slid down so far that only her eyes appeared over the dashboard. "They're leaving."

Nick turned his gaze back to the restaurant, tilting his head to the side when Marla and Steven pointed themselves toward the sidewalk rather than a vehicle. "I think they walked."

Maddie followed the twosome with her eyes, drawing back up to her full height only after they'd disappeared down the sidewalk. "Maybe we should follow on foot."

"That's not going to happen. I'm too tired."

"I could go by myself."

"That's not going to happen either." Nick's tone told Maddie he meant business. "We're sticking together ... and in the truck."

Maddie made an annoyed sound in the back of her throat. "Fine." She waited a beat and then gestured toward the road. "We need to follow them and see where they're going."

"I'm sure they're going back to the hotel."

"Then we need to follow them."

"But ... why?"

"Because I said so." Maddie was overly gruff but she didn't care. "I want to see where they go ... and what they do."

"Ugh. You're getting awfully bossy these days, Maddie. I would like to say I don't like it but, in truth, it kind of turns me on."

Maddie snickered. "Men are such simple creatures sometimes."

"We are indeed."

NICK WAS RIGHT. Marla and Steven headed straight back to the hotel, not once glancing over their shoulders to see if they were being followed. Nick parked across the street, convinced Maddie would watch them walk into the building and then happily head home.

Instead, Maddie threw open the passenger door and hopped out onto the pavement. She was already halfway across the street before Nick killed his engine, pocketed his keys, and caught up with her.

"What do you think you're doing?" Nick hissed, struggling to keep up with her energetic stride. "There's no way we can watch what's about to happen in his room ... and I have no interest in seeing that, for the record."

"I have no interest in seeing that either," Maddie said dryly as she tugged on the hotel door. "Besides, I don't think they're going up to his room. Even Marla doesn't work that fast."

"I beg to differ."

Maddie narrowed her eyes. "Do you know that from personal experience or gossip?"

"Oh, don't make me gag." Nick followed Maddie into the hotel lobby, keeping his voice low. "Marla doesn't discriminate and the guys she picks to roll around with aren't exactly the quiet type. Everyone who has ever nailed her likes to get drunk in the beer tent at festivals and talk about it."

"That is disgusting." Maddie searched the lobby, puffing out her chest when her gaze landed on the small bar to the right. Steven and Marla were already seated, and completely into one another. "Ha!"

Nick tamped down his irritation, but just barely. "Fine. They're in the bar instead of the bedroom. That doesn't mean they won't end up there eventually."

"And I don't care about that."

"What do you care about?"

"I want to know what they're talking about."

Nick was exasperated. "Mad, we can't exactly explain why we're here. If we go into that bar with the express purpose of eavesdropping, they're going to know."

"Oh, that's what you think." Maddie calmly patted Nick's cheek and then turned in the opposite direction of the bar at the same moment her father hit the main floor. "Hi, Dad. We thought we would treat you to a drink and some conversation in the bar."

If George was surprised by Maddie's sudden appearance, he didn't show it. "That sounds great." He beamed at Nick as he approached. "This is a nice surprise."

Nick was understandably suspicious. "Did she call and tell you to meet us down here?"

George chuckled, keeping his voice low. "She texted and said you were on a secret mission and needed my help."

"That figures." Nick shook his head as Maddie headed toward the quaint drinking area. "She is full of herself tonight."

"You say that like it's a bad thing," George said. "I thought you liked it when she was full of herself. In fact, one of the first serious conversations we shared revolved around Maddie's growing sense of self. You said you were happy she was gaining in the self-esteem department."

Nick's stare was withering. "Oh, that you remember, huh? You just had to bring that up."

George sobered. "You look tired."

"I am tired."

"A drink will perk you right up," Maddie called out from the door. "Come on. They have a booth ready for us."

"Fine." Nick was resigned to a night of spying and shenanigans. "You're going to owe me big time whenever we get a chance to be alone again, though. I'm warning you now."

Maddie's smile was serene. "I'm fine with that."

Oddly enough, when he saw that smile, Nick was fine with it, too.

"SO, WHO ARE WE SPYING ON?"

George sipped his bourbon and got comfortable in the booth across from Maddie and Nick. He was genuinely amused by the entire ordeal and couldn't wait to get caught up on the gossip.

"Marla and Steven." Maddie picked a booth that wasn't close enough that their conversation could be easily overheard, especially by their quarry, but near enough that she had a clear view. Ultimately that meant she couldn't hear what they said, but she didn't want to appear too obvious. "We want to know what they're up to."

George tilted his head to the side as he regarded the duo, who seemed to be deep in thought and oblivious to everyone else in the bar. "I think he's staying here."

"He is," Nick confirmed, resting his arm across the back of the booth as he lingered over a beer. He wasn't in the mood to drink, although that was mostly because he was in the mood for bed. Until Maddie got her way, though, he knew he wouldn't be seeing his pillow so he was determined to get through the night with minimal fuss. "He's also the nephew of the woman who died in the fire up by us the other day."

"Mildred Wilkins." George bobbed his head. "I've been on the phone with a local real estate woman twice this week to see about buying the land."

Nick arched an eyebrow. "Maddie mentioned that, but I didn't know you were serious."

"I am." George surveyed Nick for a long beat. "Will that upset you? I mean, if I move that close, will you be uncomfortable?"

It was an honest question so Nick felt his future father-in-law deserved an honest answer. "As long as you don't come over every day ... or develop a habit of not knocking ... I think we'll be fine. In fact, I think it would be an ideal situation in a lot of ways."

Maddie was relieved by Nick's answer but intrigued by the caveat. "How so?"

"Well, we'll be having kids of our own one day," Nick pointed out. "By the time that happens, it will be nice to know George is close and ready to serve as an emergency babysitter."

George snorted at the wicked gleam in Nick's eye. "If you think that's going to scare me away, it's not going to work. I'm looking forward to being a hands-on grandfather." He cleared his throat, discomfort obvious. "I wasn't a hands-on father so I would like to make up for at least a little bit of that by being a better grandfather."

"Oh." Maddie grinned. "That sounds good. I don't think we're going to have kids right away, though. I'd actually like to be married a year or so before we take the next step ... just so we can spend time with each other."

"I think that's a good thing," George said. "You're still young. There's no rush. Also, you two appear to enjoy each other's company. I think that will bode well for a long and happy marriage."

"I think so, too." Maddie glanced at Nick. "That's the plan, right?"

"Oh, that's already set in stone," Nick teased. "We've been destined for this since kindergarten. There's no force on this planet – and that includes your insistence on spying – that will rip us apart."

"Oh, so cute." Maddie poked his side as Nick squirmed. "As for the spying, it's necessary. The more I learn about that guy, the more I don't trust him. I just can't figure out what he has to do with all this."

George went back to staring at Steven and Marla. "I'm not sure what I can offer by way of information. I know that he checked in yesterday and there was a mild kerfuffle over it."

"How do you know that?" Nick asked, his interest piqued.

"Because he didn't want to give them a credit card. He wanted to pay cash. As everyone knows, though, you still need a credit card in case damage is done to the room or something. He didn't want to hand one over."

"Did he eventually put a credit card on file?"

George nodded. "Yeah. He was ticked, but he did it. I don't see where he had a lot of choices. He was on the phone for a bit and it was my assumption he tried to find another hotel where he wouldn't need a credit card, but he eventually went back to the front desk and allowed them to run his card."

"Hmm." Nick rubbed his chin, thoughtful. "Maybe I'll swing back by here tomorrow and see if there's anything funky about the card. Now that Margo is running this place full time, though, I'm sure she'll want me to go through her rather than one of her workers."

"That's probably true." Maddie sipped her cocktail. "Have you talked to him at all?"

"Actually, I talked to him for a few minutes this morning," George admitted. "We sat at the same table over breakfast. I got the last newspaper and he wanted to share it."

"What section did he want to read?" Nick asked, although he was convinced he already knew the answer.

"The news section. He wanted to know if there was any additional information on the fire. He was infuriated when nothing showed up other than a brief mentioning the investigation was ongoing."

"It's a Traverse City newspaper," Maddie argued. "They barely pay any attention to us. Of course there won't be constant updates. I don't expect them to run another story until an arrest is made in Mildred's death."

"I don't know anything about that," George hedged. "He was annoyed there wasn't more information, though. I suggested he go to the police station to ask questions, but he didn't seem to like that idea."

"I don't doubt that." Nick was so focused on the other table – Steven in particular – that he didn't realize Marla was staring at him until it was too late to avert his gaze. "Uh-oh."

"Uh-oh, what?" Maddie widened her eyes when she realized Marla was on her feet. "Oh, that."

"Yes, *that*." Nick remained calm as Marla stomped over, his true interest remaining back at her table where Steven sat and watched the show. He didn't make a move to join Marla, which Nick found beyond interesting. "Hello, Marla," he boomed, adopting a faux welcoming persona. "How are you doing this fine and frisky evening?"

Marla made a puckered face that reminded Nick of the sourest lemon. "Are you trying to be funny?"

"I am," Nick replied without hesitation. "Before deciding to be a cop, I considered a career in clowning. No joke. I wanted to dress up in pancake makeup and squirt roses on people. Ultimately law enforcement won out but part of my soul still longs for the big top."

Maddie involuntarily shuddered. "Oh, now I'm going to have nightmares."

Nick was amused despite himself. "I'll protect you from the evil clowns in your dreams. I promise."

"I don't even know what you guys are talking about half the time," Marla complained. "I mean ... clowns? What does that have to do with anything."

"I have no idea," Nick deadpanned. "For some reason, when I saw you, a clown popped into my head."

"Pennywise," Maddie muttered under her breath, causing George to hide a laugh with a cough.

"Do you need something, Marla?" Nick queried pointedly. "We're trying to have a nice night and that's impossible when you're around."

"I want to know why you're here," Marla replied, indignant. "I want to know if you're following me."

Nick spared a quick glance for Steven and found the man intently watching the interplay. "Why would we follow you?"

"Why would you be here otherwise?"

Nick gestured toward George while offering a "well, duh" expression that he was certain would put Marla's teeth on edge. "We're here to see George. You know, Maddie's father. He's currently living here."

"Oh, well … ." Marla briefly glared at George, as if it was somehow his fault that she looked like a raving lunatic. "Why did you come tonight, though?"

"Because I'll be out of town for a few days starting this weekend and I called them for some quality time before I go," George interjected smoothly. "I like to keep them apprised of my travel plans so they don't worry."

"I see." Marla fidgeted as she glanced over her shoulder before linking her fingers in front of her. "Well, I guess you should carry on then."

"Thank you for your permission," Nick snarked, waiting until Marla was gone and back at her table before continuing. "Okay, Mad, you might have sold me on Steven being up to something. He very clearly sent Marla over here for information."

"How can you be sure of that?" George asked.

"Because he's as suspicious of us as we are of him." Nick went back to lightly rubbing Maddie's back. "He's not interested in Marla. Not the way he wants her to believe he is, at least. He's interested in information."

"So, how does he play into this?" George asked. "Do you think he's responsible for killing Mildred?"

Nick shrugged. "Let's just say I can't rule him out."

"Does he have an alibi?"

"I have no idea," Nick replied before swigging from his beer. "We didn't ask him for an alibi. He was a shirttail nephew with no ties to the victim other than blood when we first questioned him. I think things have changed a bit on that front."

"Will you question him again?"

"Most definitely." Nick leaned over and gave Maddie a quick kiss on the temple. "You were right again, Mad. I've learned my lesson and will never question your instincts again."

Maddie beamed. "I told you."

"You're beautiful and wise."

"Ugh." George made a face. "You guys kind of make me want to gag."

"That's almost always our intent," Nick said. "Get used to that."

"Definitely get used to that," Maddie agreed. "We plan to be this way forever."

"And ever and ever," Nick enthused, earning the evil eye from George. "What? We're seriously not going to stop doing it. You need to get over it."

George was resigned. "I think I need another drink."

18. EIGHTEEN

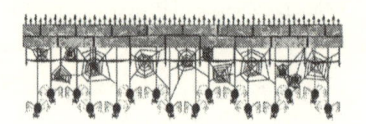

Maddie remained close to Nick when she woke the next morning, taking a few moments to bask in his warmth before facing the day. Her dreams had been busy, leaving her feeling restless and a little bit drained when she opened her eyes.

She also had a plan. Unfortunately for her, it was a plan she was certain that Nick wouldn't appreciate.

"I can hear the gears grinding from here, Mad." Nick shifted, exhaling heavily before opening one eye so he could peer at her. "You're thinking so loud you're liable to wake the dead."

Maddie pursed her lips. "That would be nice, huh? If I could wake the dead rather than just talk to them."

"I'm fine with what you can do now," Nick countered, tugging Maddie closer so he could snuggle with her. "You're always so warm and cuddly in the morning. I think that's my favorite part of the day."

In truth, it was Maddie's favorite part of the day, too. "I love you, Nicky."

Instead of responding in kind, Nick groaned. "Oh, man. You're about to butter me up for something I don't like, aren't you?"

Maddie was understandably offended. "That's an awful thing to say about the woman you're going to marry."

"It's only awful if it's not true."

"Good point." Maddie licked her lips as she pulled back her head far enough that she could stare into Nick's eyes. "I have an idea."

"Oh, I'm going to hate this." Nick pressed his eyes shut. "In fact, I think it would be better if we went back to sleep and forgot this ever happened. It can be a dream – a bad one – and we'll move on to something else. How does that sound?"

Maddie opted for honesty. "Unlikely."

"Ugh. I just knew you were going to say that." Nick had barely started the day and he already feared he was at his limit. "What is going through that busy brain of yours?"

"I told you. I have an idea."

Nick waited a beat. When Maddie didn't expand, he decided to press her on the issue. "Would you like to share it with the class?"

"Not if you're going to be a butthead."

"I'm never a butthead."

"Rarely," Maddie agreed. "What you lack in quantity, though, you make up in quality when the mood hits."

Nick didn't want to laugh. It was the exact wrong reaction. He couldn't stop himself from doing just that, though. "You are my favorite person in the world. You really are." He swooped down and smacked a loud kiss against her lips. "I can't get enough of you."

Maddie smiled at his reaction. "I feel the same way about you. You're not going to distract me from telling you about my idea, though, so it's probably unwise to try."

"Fair enough." Nick ran a hand through his morning-tousled hair. "What's your idea?"

"You gave it to me actually." Maddie rolled so she was on her back and staring at the ceiling, her eyes intense.

"I gave you the idea?" Nick remained on his side and moved his hand to her flat abdomen so he could rub away the tension he felt building there. "Well, I guess that means it must be a fantastic idea, huh?"

Maddie nodded without hesitation. "It is. I don't see why I didn't see it before."

"Okay. What's the idea?"

"I'm going to the children's home and look inside Angel's mind."

Nick remained positively still as the words washed over him. "I ... ."

"I've already made up my mind," Maddie reminded him. "You said I should be able to control whatever this is, and I think you're right. I'm going to test the theory on Angel. I felt what she was feeling the day I saved her, after all. I should be able to do it again."

Nick ran his tongue over his teeth as he debated Maddie's suggestion. "Do you think you can really see into her head?" He surprised himself with his reaction. He meant to argue with her, come up with a reason she shouldn't do it. Instead, he found himself intrigued by the prospect.

"I think it's worth a shot," Maddie replied. "I mean ... if she can show me what happened I'll be able to help her. If she's not willing to talk ... or unable to hear exactly what I'm saying ... or confused for some other reason ... I should be able to figure it out. We can't do anything until she decides to help us. We're ... stuck."

"I wouldn't go that far," Nick countered. "You're not far off, though. I'm going to chase information on Steven ... and hard ... today. We need Angel to fill in the blanks, though."

"That's why I'm heading out there as soon as I'm done with breakfast. I'm going to figure out exactly what happened to her and I'm not leaving until I do."

Nick smoothed Maddie's hair as he regarded her. "I think that sounds like a plan."

Maddie's eyes glinted with suspicion. "You're not going to try and talk me out of this."

"No."

"Why?"

"Because you're the smartest woman I know and if you feel this is going to lead us to answers, I have to agree with you. There's a reason you get these feelings you get. It's because you have an inner sense that's trying to guide you. I'm not going to ask you to start ignoring those feelings, though."

Maddie exhaled heavily, relieved. "Thank you."

"Besides, there's a uniformed officer standing guard at the children's home," Nick added. "You'll be safe there. I would much rather you spend your day at the children's home than running around the woods looking for a ghost."

"I should be angry about you saying that, but I'm going to let it slide."

"I think that's best for everybody," Nick agreed.

"I'm still going to be irritated later."

"I can live with that."

"I might punish you."

"I can definitely live with that."

Maddie snorted at the innocent expression on his face. "You're kind of a pervert sometimes. Has anyone ever told you that?"

Nick's eyes gleamed. "The question is, can you live with that?"

The smile on Maddie's face was so wide it almost swallowed her pleasing features. "I think somehow I'll manage to muddle through."

"Good to know."

"I thought so."

KRESKIN WAS ALREADY AT his desk when Nick entered their shared office two hours later. The older police officer's attention was on his computer and he didn't as much as look up when Nick entered.

"Are you looking at porn?" Nick asked dryly.

Kreskin rolled his eyes. "Yes. I started my shift an hour early to look at porn. You caught me."

Nick recognized the edge in Kreskin's voice and wisely decided to step carefully. "What's going on?"

"A couple of hikers found a car abandoned in the woods about four miles out of town," Kreskin replied. "It was an older Ford and someone went through the trouble to cover the car with branches as a form of camouflage."

Nick was confused. "I guess I don't understand."

"The car belongs to a woman named Carrie Grimes."

"I still don't understand."

"Carrie Grimes is married to a man named Michael Grimes," Kreskin volunteered. "She's been missing for almost a month. The car that was just discovered has probably been out there all that time. It was found by that small inlet that leads to the lake. It's off the road a bit and can't be easily seen. Since it's so early in the season, people aren't visiting the lake yet so ... it literally could've been there the entire month."

Nick wrinkled his forehead. "Michael Grimes. Why does that name sound familiar?"

"I ran it. The only Michael Grimes I can find legally changed his name to Steven Wilkins several years ago."

Things slipped into place for Nick. "Oh, good grief. Steven is Michael."

"And his wife is missing," Kreskin added. "Her family reported her missing four weeks ago. That was after she seemingly moved out of her house and only contacted them sporadically over a two-week period."

"But ... what would she be doing here?" Nick was talking more to himself than Kreskin. It was his partner who answered, though.

"That road is behind your house," Kreskin pointed out. "It's also behind Mildred's house."

"What do we know about Carrie Grimes?" Nick asked, straightening his shoulders.

"Not a lot as of yet," Kreskin replied. "We know that she married Michael Grimes sixteen years ago. We know that Michael Grimes changed his name to Steven Wilkins after that. We also know that Carrie Grimes gave birth to a daughter about a year after she married."

Oxygen escaped Nick's lungs with a whoosh. "Angel."

"Actually, the girl's name was Angelina Grimes," Kreskin replied. "I can't find any photos of her online that don't date back to when she was a toddler but ... I'm going to guess we've found our girl."

Nick slid into his desk chair, his mind moving at a fantastic rate.

"Angel is Michael Grimes' daughter. Michael Grimes was Mildred's nephew. Forty years ago, Mildred helped her sister-in-law escape her abusive husband and go into hiding. She took her son with her. That son reconnected with his father years after the fact and apparently didn't believe the stories his mother told. Now his wife is missing, his aunt was found dead, and his daughter is locked up in a place where he can't get his hands on her."

"Pretty much," Kreskin confirmed. "I don't think this is a coincidence. He seemed uninterested in what was going on when we first questioned him. He told a nice story but wasn't engaged. Then, suddenly, you mention finding Angel and he turns up in town. There has to be a reason behind that."

Nick finally understood what that reason was. "I took a photo of Steven at the bar last night. Maddie is at the children's home. I'm going to message it to her and have her show it around. If we can get confirmation that Steven is behind this, we can grab him at the hotel before he has a chance to leave for the day."

"That sounds like a plan to me."

PATTY AND SHARON WERE outside the observation window when Maddie was cleared through security. She joined them and already had a story ready to explain her appearance.

"I'm just going to sit with her a bit," Maddie announced, keeping her face placid even though her heart was thumping. She wasn't the best liar. That's one of the reasons she was always so fearful about people finding out about her gift. "I think she will eventually have to react to me."

"So, you're just going to wait her out?" Sharon obviously wasn't impressed with Maddie's suggestion. "Do you really think that's going to work?"

Maddie shrugged. "Do you have a better idea?"

"We've got a specialist coming from Detroit," Patty supplied. "She's hopefully going to be able to make some headway."

"And when does she arrive?"

"Not for a few hours."

"That means there's no reason I can't sit with Angel until then," Maddie pointed out. "It can't possibly do any harm."

Patty and Sharon exchanged a weighted look.

"I guess that's okay," Sharon said after a beat. "She hasn't eaten since yesterday, which I don't think is healthy given her weight. If you could force some food down her, that would be great."

"Get me a tray." Maddie kept her smile in place. "I have a good feeling about today. In fact ... ." She broke off when her phone dinged, barely managing to keep a scowl at bay as she dug for it. "Hmm." She studied the message Nick sent her and touched the attached photo before lifting her phone. "Is this the guy who was here yesterday?"

Sharon flicked her eyes to the screen and stared hard. "I can't be sure, but I think that's him. I mean ... I'm about seventy-five percent sure that's him. That photo is kind of dark – clearly in a bar or something – so I can't be a hundred percent sure."

"But you're reasonably sure it's him," Maddie pressed.

Sharon nodded. "Yes."

"Who is he?" Patty asked as Maddie began typing on her phone. "Do you know who he is?"

"Yes, and it's a weird story," Maddie replied. "Basically he's Mildred's nephew." She frowned at her phone as another message came through.

"That's the woman Angel refers to as her grandmother, right?" Sharon queried.

Maddie bobbed her head. "Huh. This is weird."

"What?"

"Nick sent another photo to see if I recognized it." Maddie turned her thoughtful eyes to the girl hiding in the corner on the other side of the window. "He thinks it might be a photo of Angel's mother."

Patty's interest piqued. "Has he found her? I think her mother would definitely help in this situation."

Maddie swallowed hard. "No. They found her car."

"That doesn't sound good," Sharon noted. "Is Angel's mother

dead? How did Mildred get her if the mother is dead? For that matter, why would Mildred hide Angel from her own nephew?"

Maddie had a sinking suspicion that she knew exactly why Mildred would go out of her way to hide Angel. "I need to talk to her. It's probably best I do it right now. Nick is on his way to pick up Steven, which is a good thing, but we still need answers."

"So, talk to her," Sharon suggested. "If anyone can get through to her, it's you."

"I hope that's true."

MADDIE'S SMILE DIDN'T PROMISE laughter when she entered the room. Angel, as if hearing a noise, flicked her eyes to the door. She didn't cringe at the sight of Maddie. She didn't excitedly throw herself at her either.

"Hello, Angel."

Angel turned her attention forward and began studying her knees. Maddie knew she had limited time so she opted not to wait for Angel to come to her. It was time to go to Angel ... and demand answers, if it became necessary.

Maddie sat on the floor in front of Angel, giving the girl no choice but to look directly at her. She clutched her phone to her chest and debated how to start. Ultimately Maddie decided to get right to the heart of matters.

"Is this your mother?" Maddie extended the phone so Angel could see the woman in question.

Angel's countenance was pouty when she dragged her eyes to the phone. Her expression shifted quickly when she straightened and grabbed the phone, her eyes never leaving the photograph.

"That's her, isn't it?" Maddie felt mildly sick to her stomach. She recognized the woman in the photo. It was the same face she saw the day Mildred's house caught fire, the same woman who led Maddie to Angel. The same woman who was very obviously dead because she was walking around as a ghost. "What were you doing at Mildred's house?"

Angel didn't look away from the phone.

"I think we've got some of it figured out," Maddie supplied. "I know about your mother. I know that Mildred was your father's aunt. I know that Mildred once helped your grandmother – your father's mother – escape from an abusive husband. I also know that your grandmother didn't share everything with me when I questioned her."

Angel remained still, but Maddie sensed a bit of give in the way the girl reacted to her.

"Your father abused you, didn't he?"

Nothing.

"He abused your mother, too." Maddie was mostly talking to herself, but she had a feeling Angel was either listening or understood on some level Maddie couldn't quite grasp. "Your mother decided to run and either your grandmother pointed her toward Mildred or your mother knew the stories herself and asked for help.

"It's not as easy to hide these days," she continued. "Mildred couldn't simply put you and your mother up in a house one town over and get away with it. To buy time, you guys were staying with her, right?"

Angel didn't answer, but her eyes were now trained on Maddie.

"Your mother disappeared at some point, didn't she?" Maddie questioned. "Mildred knew something happened to her and it was only a matter of time before someone came for you. I don't understand why she put you in the basement, locked you in there, but she must have had a reason.

"Your father is the one who came to Mildred's house the other day," she continued. "He's the one who broke in and killed Mildred. He's the one who started the fire. I think he was looking for you and either didn't realize you were in the house or didn't care. That's only one of the things I can't figure out."

Angel licked her lips but otherwise remained still.

"I need to know, Angel." Maddie instinctively reached out and grabbed the girl's hand. "You don't have to tell me what happened. You just have to let me see."

Maddie squeezed the girl's hand tightly when she tried to pull away.

"Let me see," Maddie repeated. "You have no idea how important this is. Just ... you don't have to talk. You don't have to sign. All you have to do is let me in."

If Angel understood what Maddie was suggesting, she didn't show it. Ironically, though, she let Maddie do exactly what she asked. She opened her mind as Maddie slid inside.

She showed her everything she remembered from the time she was a small child until the moment Maddie rescued her. She allowed Maddie to live through years of anguish, although it only took Maddie seconds to see everything.

Even as the images overwhelmed her, Maddie dug deeper. She looked harder. It was only then that she saw everything ... and the true horror of one family became all too real.

19. NINETEEN

"**A**re you sure he left?"
Nick and Kreskin were frustrated upon arrival at the hotel and being informed that Steven had already checked out. That's where George found them a few minutes later and he was understandably confused.

"I actually didn't see him leave, but I heard the maids talking and they said that he left his room a mess," George replied. "Apparently he had some sort of fit yesterday and broke a vase and threw a few things across the room. They said they understood why he didn't want to leave his credit card on file if this was how he always intended to leave the room."

"He didn't want to leave his credit card on file because he didn't want a record of staying in town," Nick corrected. "I don't understand why he stayed only to pick up and leave before anything is settled, though."

"What do you think he wants to settle?" George asked.

"You're behind," Nick realized. "You don't know. That makes sense. How could you know?"

"Know what?"

"Steven has a wife who conveniently went missing," Kreskin

supplied. "Her car was found hidden behind Mildred's house. He also has a daughter, who is fifteen."

Things slid into place for George. "A daughter who Maddie found."

"A daughter who is protected at the children's home," Nick clarified. "Maddie is out there with her now."

"Maybe he recognized that he couldn't get close to Angel since he failed on the first attempt," George suggested. "Maybe he thought it was better to cut and run."

Nick immediately started shaking his head. "No. I don't think that's right. He has another plan."

"What plan?" Kreskin was legitimately curious. "What do you think he's going to do?"

Nick could only come up with one answer. "He's going to the children's home. He's going to make his last stand there because he's determined to get Angel. She's the thing he's focused on."

"But ... there's a police officer on the premises."

"And maybe Steven doesn't care." Nick's stomach twisted. "We have to get out there and offer some support. In fact, now that Steven knows where Angel is, we should probably move her to another location."

"I don't know that we have the authority to do that, but we can try."

"Let's get out there." Nick moved to leave the hotel but stopped long enough to offer George reassurance. "Maddie will be fine. I'll make sure of it."

George nodded, uncertain. "Call me when you get there. I want to know she's safe."

"You've got it."

MADDIE FOUGHT TO CATCH her breath as the cascading visions washed over her. *It's too much.* That's all she could think as ugly image after ugly image barreled into her brain to take up residence. *It's too much.*

Angel, her eyes wide and fearful, watched Maddie as if she were a bomb about to go off.

When Maddie finally found her voice, she gripped Angel's hand as tightly as possible and began to nod. "I understand."

"And what is it you understand?"

Maddie stiffened at the voice, the hair on the back of her neck standing on end as she slowly turned to face the door.

It wasn't Sharon standing there asking questions. It wasn't Patty with her magical hands. They were both absent, and Maddie had no doubt it was due to the man standing in the opening with a knife in his hand. In quick succession, Maddie realized several things. The first of which was that Steven Wilkins had somehow managed to make it past the police officer at the door and the two women who were supposed to be standing outside the window. The second was that the knife blade was covered with blood. The third was there was no second exit for the room. She was trapped and the only way out was through Steven.

To her utter surprise, Maddie blew out an extended breath and lessened her grip on Angel. She had no idea how to handle the situation, but she was the only one who could so she had to figure a way out. When faced with the knowledge that failure isn't an option, all one can do is succeed. That's what Maddie told herself as she slowly got to her feet.

"Did you kill the policeman by the door?"

Steven's smirk was evil. "He didn't even see it coming. I bought some roses from the store on the highway and acted like a deliveryman. By the time he realized what was happening, it was already too late."

Maddie swallowed hard. It was clear the man was deranged. That would make things more difficult. "And Patty and Sharon?"

"Are those the two women who were on the other side of the window?"

Maddie nodded.

"Let's just say they're otherwise engaged and leave it at that, huh?" Steven shifted his eyes to a cowering Angel. She hadn't as much as made a noise since he entered, but Maddie could sense the overt terror ripping through the girl. "Hello, honey. Daddy is here. I've finally found you. It's time to go home."

Angel turned her face to stare at the wall and made a whimpering noise. Maddie wanted to console her, hold her until the tremors subsided, but she couldn't risk that. Steven had a distinct physical advantage over her and it would only be compounded if she made herself small and hid in the corner.

"I don't think she wants to go with you," Maddie supplied. "Perhaps you should try again another time when she's not so overwrought."

Steven kept his eyes on his daughter. "She wants to go with me. She loves me."

"That's not how it looks to me."

"Well, I don't care how it looks to you!" Steven exploded, his eyes lit with fury. "Did I ask how it looks to you? When I want to know your opinion, I'll ask."

Maddie refused to react out of fear. If Steven recognized exactly how terrified she really was he would take advantage of the situation. All she had going for her at the present moment was his uncertainty. He had no way of knowing how she would react.

"I know what you are," Maddie intoned, hoping she sounded creepy and put together. "I know what you did."

"Oh, really?" Steven rolled his eyes. "What am I?"

"A sociopath."

"That seems like too easy of an answer."

Maddie couldn't argue with that. So, because she needed time to think, she decided to buy it with her mouth.

"You were raised by a mother who tried to give you everything," Maddie started. "Penny – or should I say Priscilla – realized right away she couldn't raise another child with your father. She went to your aunt and the two women devised a plan to get away.

"It was much easier back then," she continued. "The information age wasn't quite upon us. I'm sure she needed a little help to create new identities, but somehow she did it and you and your mother were safe."

"My mother was a nutball who made stuff up," Steven argued. "She was a bitter old shrew who wanted to punish my father for no good reason."

"That's what he told you," Maddie argued. "By the time you met him he was already sick. He didn't look scary because he didn't have the strength to pull it off. You were a boy in need of a father figure and you found one who was a master at twisting minds.

"I mean, he convinced you to change your name and turn on your mother," she continued. "He convinced you to embrace his evil legacy even though you could've had a better life. This was after you married Carrie, though, of course. This was after you started a family of your own."

Steven looked momentarily shaken but he returned to his menacing form relatively quickly. "You don't know anything about Carrie."

"I know she's dead."

"Really? How do you know that?"

Maddie thought about the sad and morose ghost she saw outside Mildred's house the day of the fire. She stayed behind to watch her daughter. She was defeated in life, but she continued to fight for her daughter in death.

"Because you found her, although I'm not quite sure how," Maddie replied. "You found her and killed her. Her body is in the woods behind Mildred's house." Maddie took a chance that was true. Things were starting to come together rapidly in her head. "She's dead and Mildred knew something was wrong when Carrie didn't return to the house. She was hiding Angel and Carrie there while she tried to figure a way out of this mess."

"You have no idea what you're talking about," Steven spat. "Carrie got what was coming to her. She stole my child."

This was where the images Maddie saw in Angel's head came into play.

"You gave up your right to that child when you mistreated her,"

Maddie argued. "You gave up that right when you broke her mother's arm and cracked her ribs. You gave up that right when you threw Angel down the stairs. That's what caused her hearing issues, by the way. That's on you.

"Of course, because you're a monster, you only mistreated her more once it became apparent that her hearing was affected," Maddie continued. "You screamed and yelled at her, something she could make out with one ear but not the other, and when she misunderstood, you hurt her again."

Angel had given up pretending she wasn't listening. Her clear eyes were on Maddie now and she was focused on the story.

"Carrie knew some sign language from school and she got a book so Angel could learn," Maddie continued. "They hid it from you because you were happy thinking Angel couldn't communicate. In addition to damaging her hearing with that fall down the stairs, she also stopped talking. That made things so much easier for you.

"Now, I'm not sure if she can still talk, but you were convinced she couldn't and that made things easier for you," she said. "Carrie convinced Angel to pretend she couldn't talk, couldn't hear a thing, because you were more likely to leave her alone if she didn't understand what you were ranting and raving about. Carrie thought you might eventually lose interest in terrorizing her if she didn't react to what you were doing."

Even though he was full of bluster and bravado, Maddie didn't miss the way Steven's face drained of color.

"How could you possibly know that?" Steven challenged.

"Because Angel told me." Maddie was matter of fact. "She showed me everything. I know how you treated Carrie. I know what you did to Angel. I know all of it. I also know you didn't start doing it until you met your father. Apparently he groomed you in a way that I'm not sure I understand. Carrie understood, though. Your mother did, too. Even though she was loyal to you Priscilla recognized what you were turning into. She's the one who pointed Carrie toward Mildred. She's the one who helped."

Steven's cheeks flooded with color. "You're lying. My mother would never do that. She kept trying to get me back on her side after we had our falling out. She wouldn't risk that by helping Carrie."

"Oh, you're dumber than I thought." Maddie made a tsking sound in the back of her throat. "Your mother was playing you. I saw her, by the way. We had a long talk. She told me about your father and what he did to her. She told me how she fled.

"I can't help but think about how disappointed she must have been when you chose to embrace his legacy," she continued. "You had a mother who fought the odds and saved you to look at as a hero and instead you decided to be a physically abusive jerk. How she must've wondered if she should've gone with her initial urge and given you up for adoption."

Steven was flabbergasted. "You're making that up."

Maddie pressed forward despite the hatred flitting through his eyes. "I'm not. She told me she was going to give you up for adoption after she fled. She thought it might be better for you just in case your father managed to find her. Mildred pretended to be pregnant so she could be the one to give you up, but Priscilla changed her mind at the last minute. She couldn't let you go."

"You're lying!"

"I'm not." Maddie refused to back down. "You turned into the one thing your mother was desperate to keep you from becoming. I recognized she was hiding something the day I visited her. I thought it was something to do with you. I was wrong. It had nothing to do with you and everything to do with Angel.

"You see, your mother realized that as long as you were out roaming around you would be a threat to Angel," she continued. "She wanted to keep her granddaughter safe, even if that meant never seeing her again. Once Angel was a ward of the state Priscilla figured that she would be safer in someone else's house. If Priscilla took her in, you would simply find her.

"Your mother understood that you were so evil you would kill her to get to Angel," Maddie said. "In your twisted mind, Angel is your property. You don't want to love her, but you do want to control her."

"She's mine," Steven seethed. "She's my daughter and I'm taking her with me."

"No, you're not." Maddie shuffled closer to Angel in an effort to block Steven from getting close. "I'm not going to let you touch her."

"And how are you going to stop me?"

"Any way I can." Maddie was resigned to fight. "You should know, you're not the first crazy person I've come into contact with. I'm not afraid to fight you. I'll do what's necessary to keep Angel safe. You can be sure of that."

"Oh, really?" Steven's eye roll was pronounced. "Do you think you're a match for me? Do you think you can stop me from taking what's mine?"

Maddie's lips curved upwards when she felt something familiar brush against her heart. She recognized the presence right away. "I think you're not going to touch Angel. I have faith."

"Well, we'll just see how far that faith gets you." Steven took a menacing step in her direction, but he didn't make it another step. Instead, he found a tall figure behind him and a gun pressed to the center of his shoulder blades. "What the ... ?"

"If you take another step, I will kill you where you stand," Nick warned, his chest heaving. "I'm not kidding. I won't feel bad about it in the least. You're the lowest form of scum out there. I mean ... you're worse than pond scum. This world would be better without you."

Maddie swallowed hard at the fire in Nick's eyes. She remained quiet, though. Nick was the one who would have to make the ultimate choice.

"That's my daughter," Steven snapped. "She's mine. I won't let anyone take her from me."

"Then go after her," Nick suggested. "That will give me a reason to shoot you and end this once and for all."

Maddie trained her eyes on Steven's face, curious how he would react. Like the true coward he was, he ultimately dropped the knife and whined the second Nick pushed him to the ground and began cuffing him.

"You don't understand," Steven spat. "Carrie ruined everything. That's my daughter. She belongs to me."

"She doesn't belong to anyone but herself," Maddie countered as she sat on the ground and held her arms open so Angel could crawl into them. "She's her own person and the only thing I can say with any certainty is that she'll be free of you forever. That is the one thing her mother wanted and I'm going to make sure it happens."

"You've got that right, Mad." Nick winked at Angel to get her to smile. "This is over. Everyone is safe and can move forward. It's going to be better now, kid. I promise you that."

NICK FOUND MADDIE standing in front of the home an hour later. Given the emergency personnel running in and out – the assigned police officer was still alive and transferred to the hospital for emergency surgery – he hadn't been able to spend any time with her.

"Are you okay?" Nick pulled Maddie in for a hug before she could answer. "I was terrified when I saw we had an officer down when I arrived. All I could think was that I was going to kill him if he touched one hair on your head."

"He didn't get close enough." Maddie buried her face in the hollow of his neck. "I'm fine. I know everything that happened to Angel, though, and it was terrible. I don't think I'm going to ever be able to get those images out of my mind."

Sympathy rolled off Nick in waves. "We'll make sure she has a happy home so she can start making new memories. It's going to get better for her. I promise."

"She can talk, although her mother tried to make her hide it."

"Her mother did what she thought was best and second-guessing her isn't going to do anyone any good."

"Her body is somewhere in the woods behind Mildred's house."

"I already called the state police and they're out there looking." Nick stroked the back of Maddie's head as he rocked back and forth.

"Mildred should've come to us for help. I'll never understand why she didn't."

"She came from a different time."

"Meaning?"

"Meaning that trust isn't always easy."

"I guess not." Nick pressed a kiss to Maddie's forehead, raising his eyebrows when he caught sight of Sharon and Patty leading Angel out of the house. "How are you guys?"

"We're fine," Sharon replied. "He locked us in a closet. I'm more embarrassed than anything else."

"At least you're not hurt," Maddie said, turning in Nick's arms so she could focus her full attention on Angel. "You're being moved to a new location, but I promise I'm going to visit the second I'm allowed."

Angel stared at her for a long beat, her expression unreadable. Then, to absolutely everyone's surprise, she opened her mouth and spoke. "You saved me."

Maddie choked back tears at the girl's gravelly voice. She obviously hadn't been exercising her vocal cords much in the past few months. "I did what needed to be done."

Angel nodded and offered a pretty smile. "Thank you."

"You're very welcome."

20. TWENTY

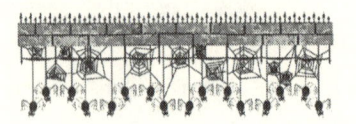

Three days later, Maddie and Nick found themselves at a fundraiser picnic for CPS, surrounded by kids and a small carnival. It was a beautiful day, the sun high in the sky, and Maddie was determined to have a good time even though worry about Angel and where she would ultimately land continued to stalk her.

"I'm surprised you agreed to come to this," Maddie admitted as she accepted a glass of lemonade from Nick. "I thought you wanted to take our first walk to the lake."

"I did but the state police are still combing the woods to make sure there's no additional evidence related to Carrie's death. Finding her body was only the beginning. I didn't think we needed a reminder of what happened on our first lake outing of the year."

Maddie sipped her lemonade and nodded. She'd seen various officers traipsing through the woods for days. Carrie's body was discovered thanks to the K-9 unit the day after the fallout at the children's home. Investigators remained behind to collect further evidence for Steven's trial, but they were due to finish soon. "I guess that makes sense. We can wait a week."

"We can," Nick agreed. "Besides, I think being here today is more important."

Something about the way he uttered the statement made Maddie suspicious. "What do you mean by that?"

"I don't mean anything by that."

"You're lying." Maddie pressed her lips together and searched his face. "You're up to something."

Nick snorted at her adorable expression. "I'm not up to anything, love. I might know something that's happening today, though, and I think it's something you need to see."

Maddie tilted her head to the side. "John didn't go ring shopping without me, did he? We're supposed to be going tomorrow. He can't pick out a ring without me. We made a deal."

Nick chuckled. "No. Christy is allowing him to sleep at her house – although only on the couch – so he wants to make sure he buys the exact right ring. He wants you for that. What's happening today has nothing to do with John and Christy."

Maddie was secretly relieved and yet nervous at the same time. "So ... what's happening today?"

"Well, for starters, Angel is here." Nick inclined his chin toward the girl. She sat at one of the picnic tables, swinging her feet as she watched the other kids play. She didn't move to join them, but she didn't look unhappy. "I thought you would be happy to spend time with her."

"I *am* happy to spend time with her," Maddie confirmed. "I've seen her every single day since it happened, though. I told you about it. She's back to mostly signing, but I think that's a trust thing. Eventually she'll start talking again."

"I'm very hopeful about that." Nick studied the angular planes of Maddie's face. "Something else is going to happen today, though, and I want you to be a witness."

"A witness to what?"

"A changing life." Nick smiled when he caught sight of two people walking across the parking lot. They were focused on the children, although one of the individuals – the older woman – seemed to sense she was being watched and turned her eyes in his direction. "Actually, I think it's more apt to say it's multiple changing lives."

Maddie glanced over her shoulder so she could determine what Nick was looking at and she raised her eyebrows when her gaze fell on Priscilla. "What's she doing here?"

"You'll see."

"But ... ." Maddie didn't get a chance to finish because the woman was heading their way, followed by a man who looked to be pushing sixty and seemed nervous and a bit out of sorts. "What's going on?"

"You'll find out." Nick rested his lemonade on a nearby table and pressed his left hand to the small of Maddie's back before reaching out to greet Priscilla with his right. "I'm glad you managed to work things out so you could visit."

"I'm glad, too." Priscilla beamed at him before allowing her smile to slip and turning to Maddie. "You're probably angry at me, huh?"

Was she? Maddie had no idea how to answer. The first night after the attack Maddie spent a good four hours fuming at Priscilla. She was convinced the woman could've fixed things if she'd only told the whole truth from the beginning. Now, she wasn't so sure.

"I'm not entirely certain how I feel about you," Maddie admitted after a beat. "I knew you were hiding something the day we met, by the way. I had no idea exactly what that something was."

"Yes, well, I really was trying to keep Angel safe," Priscilla offered. "It wasn't about me or you. It was about her."

The man with Priscilla uncomfortably cleared his throat. "I'm Edgar Grimes, by the way." He jutted out his hand, which Nick warmly shook. "I'm glad to meet you. I've heard a lot about you ... well, both of you."

"Was it good or bad?" Maddie asked.

Edgar smiled, making him look younger than his sixty years. "It was good. You've been all over the news, although I couldn't help but notice that you refused all interview requests. Most people would be all over a situation like that to get their accolades.

"Heck, there's some woman from Blackstone Bay who barely dated my brother and she's been on every news show that will have her," he continued. "She tells a harrowing story of survival even though her life was never in danger."

"Ah, yes, Marla." Nick made a face. "She likes attention. She can't seem to help herself."

"I can imagine." Edgar shifted from one foot to the other as he licked his lips and glanced back at the children. "I should probably tell you that I stopped at the county jail to see Michael. Er, I mean Steven. He's adamant that we call him Steven."

"That's because he's a psycho loser who thinks only about himself," Maddie groused.

Priscilla's expression turned dour. "If you think I'm going to be offended by that, I'm not. I have no illusions regarding Michael. Once he met his father and started to change, I realized exactly what he was turning into. I'm not proud."

"I don't think anyone could be proud of what Steven did," Edgar said gently.

"I'm not sorry for trying to protect Angel either," Priscilla added. "I've already told your boyfriend, but I think I owe you an explanation, too. I thought if Angel was safe with the state there was no way Michael could get to her. I thought they would move her to a new home and he would never be able to find her. However hard it was – and you'll never know how terrible I felt – I thought I was doing right by her."

Maddie had pretty much figured out that portion of the story herself. What she hadn't figured out was the bigger picture. "And Carrie? You had to at least suspect that Steven killed her. Who were you protecting by keeping that information to yourself?"

"Not Michael," Priscilla replied without hesitation. "When Carrie first went missing I was confused. I thought maybe she found a new place to live and was figuring things out. It was only after two days that Mildred and I realized something bad happened to her. Then we were in a real pickle, though."

"I knew you and Mildred were probably working together," Maddie muttered. "There was no way it all made sense unless you were a team."

"Yes, well, you're smart." Priscilla's smile was small and didn't make it all the way to her eyes. "When Carrie disappeared we figured we knew what happened but had no proof. We didn't know what to do. We were making arrangements to move Angel out of Mildred's house when the fire broke out."

"You mean when Steven set the fire," Maddie corrected. "I still don't understand why he would do that knowing Angel was in the house."

"He didn't know. Mildred put a lock on Angel's door that was outside the room so she could pretend it was a storeroom should Michael somehow find his way inside. Actually, before we moved Angel in it was a storeroom.

"That situation was only supposed to be temporary," Priscilla continued. "You have to understand. We thought it would take a few days to get settled. It's not as easy to hide someone as it used to be."

Despite her anger, Maddie couldn't help feeling sorry for Priscilla. The situation was hard on everybody. Steven was a monster of epic proportions, but Priscilla tried to do right by her granddaughter. That was the most important thing.

"I'm not blaming you," Maddie said finally. "I understand how difficult things were and how you were struggling. Carrie would still be alive, though, if you'd gone to the police."

"I understand that. Back in my day, though, Steven Sr. was friends with the men on the police force. They knew what was happening – there were only two of them, mind you – and did nothing to stop it. They looked past me and remained friends with my husband. I didn't think I could trust them."

"I hope you feel differently now," Nick prodded. "If you'd told us what was happening from the beginning we could've ended this a lot quicker – and without as much bloodshed. We got lucky that the officer stationed at the children's home is going to be okay. Things could've gone much worse, though."

"I understand that." Priscilla smoothed the front of her blazer. "I can't apologize enough. I'm sorry for what Michael did."

Maddie believed her. "What are you going to do about Angel?"

"That's actually why we're here," Edgar said. "My wife and I have an empty house. All of our kids are grown and gone. We've been in contact with the state, talking about Angel's specific needs for the hearing and speech problems, and we've already got classes and outpatient care set up for her."

Maddie wasn't certain she understood what the man was saying. "You're taking her?"

Edgar bobbed his head. "We are. My mother wanted to do it but, due to age, we feel our home is the better fit. Mom will be able to visit regularly but my wife and I are better suited to keep Angel on the schedule she needs."

"So, she's moving to Bellaire?" Maddie tapped on her bottom lip as she considered the development. "That's not far away from Blackstone Bay."

Priscilla smirked as she exchanged a quick look with Nick. "Yes, well, I've been informed you'll want to visit on a regular basis, too. This is a convenient move for that, wouldn't you say?"

Even though part of her wanted to hold onto the anger she'd been hoarding like gold, Maddie knew it was a waste of time. "So, you're really taking her?" Despite herself, she could see endless possibilities in front of Angel. "You're going to get her the help she needs and a nice home?"

"More than that, we're going to love her," Edgar promised. "I didn't get a chance to know her mother well because of everything going on. I saw her a few times, but Steven was always odd. He was better in youth, although that sweetness he had as a child faded away.

"I'm going to make sure that Angel doesn't lose her sweetness," he continued. "I'm going to give her the best life I can. I owe her mother for it."

"We both owe her mother," Priscilla corrected. "We're going to do our very best by her."

Maddie chewed her bottom lip as she flicked her eyes to Nick. "You knew about this and didn't tell me?"

Nick shrugged. "I found out that everything was coming together this morning. It's not as if I hid it from you for a long time. I thought you would enjoy the surprise."

Maddie's lips curved up. "It's definitely a surprise."

"A good surprise?"

"Yes." Maddie bobbed her head and turned to stare at Angel. The girl was trying to act calm and disengaged, but it was obvious she recognized Priscilla. There was interest carved on her face ... and hope. "I think this is the best way to spend a weekend day ever."

Nick chuckled as he slid an arm around her shoulders and kissed her forehead. "I think you're right. There's nothing better than a picnic."

"Definitely." Maddie briefly shut her eyes. "Now, I think I smell hot dogs. Who's up for some food and then a nice get-to-know-you session?"

Priscilla was clearly tickled with Maddie's determination to take over the meet and greet. "That sounds like a nice way to start the spring."

"Absolutely," Nick agreed. "Let's get to it, shall we?"

It wasn't a perfect ending, but it was a wonderful start, Maddie mused as they crossed the lawn. No one could ask for more than that.

Made in the USA
Coppell, TX
24 November 2023